RACE FOR THE SKY

RACE
FOR THE SKY

The Kitty Hawk Diaries of Johnny Moore

DAN GUTMAN

SIMON & SCHUSTER BOOKS FOR YOUNG READERS

New York London Toronto Sydney Singapore

SIMON & SCHUSTER BOOKS FOR YOUNG READERS
An imprint of Simon & Schuster Children's Publishing Division
1230 Avenue of the Americas, New York, New York 10020
Copyright © 2003 by Dan Gutman
SIMON & SCHUSTER BOOKS FOR YOUNG READERS is a trademark of Simon & Schuster.
Book design by Greg Stadnyk
The text for this book is set in Century Oldstyle, Trixie, Clarendon, and Rosewood.
Photographs courtesy of the Library of Congress and Dan Gutman
Maps on pages 8 and 12 by Nina Wallace
Manufactured in the United States of America
4 6 8 10 9 7 5 3
Library of Congress Cataloging-in-Publication Data
Gutman, Dan.
Race for the sky : the Kitty Hawk diaries of Johnny Moore / Dan Gutman.—1st ed.
p. cm.
Based on the real-life story of Johnny Moore.
Summary: Ordered to practice his writing skills in the blank book his mother gave him, fourteen-
year-old Johnny would rather go fishing near his home on North Carolina's Outer Banks and cannot
think of anything important to write until two "dingbatters" from Ohio arrive in 1900 and try to
build a flying machine.
ISBN 0-689-84554-5
1. Wright, Wilbur, 1867–1912—Juvenile fiction. 2. Wright, Orville, 1871-1948—Juvenile fiction.
[1. Wright, Wilbur, 1867–1912—Fiction. 2. Wright, Orville, 1871-1948—Fiction. 3. Flight—Fiction.
4. Outer Banks (N.C.)—History—20th century—Fiction. 5. Diaries—Fiction.] I. Title.
PZ7.G9846 Rac 2003
[Fic]—dc21   2003011527

Dedicated to all the great kids at schools I visited in 2002...

In New Jersey: Mansion Avenue School in Audubon; Chittick, Frost, and Solomon Schechter in East Brunswick; Ocean Road in Point Pleasant; West Dover in Toms River; Woodbury Heights in Woodbury Heights; Jefferson and Wilson in Westfield; Edison in Westmont; Glenwood in Short Hills; Orchard Hill in Belle Mead; Ocean Avenue in Middletown; Saddle River Day in Saddle River; Upper Freehold Regional in Allentown; Olson Middle in Tabernacle; Sandshore in Mount Olive; Hewit in Ringwood; Roosevelt in Garfield; Hillside in Bridgewater; Durand in Vineland; Whitman in Turnersville; Jaggard in Marlton; Burnet Hill in Livingston; Seth Boyden in Maplewood; Normandy Park in Morristown; and Moriah School in Englewood

In Pennsylvania: Holtzman School in Harrisburg; Houserville and Park Forest in State College; Boyce Middle in Upper Saint Clair; Abington Friends in Jenkintown; and Welch School in Newtown

In Illinois: Timber Ridge Middle School in Plainfield; Sullivan, Eisenhower, and MacArthur Schools in Prospect Heights; Country Meadows and Kildeer in Long Grove; Ivy Hall and Prairie in Buffalo Grove; and Forest Hills, Field Park, and Laidlaw in Western Springs

In Virginia: Poplar Tree, Virginia Run, Westbriar, and Newington Forest Schools in Fairfax County; and North Tazewell, Abbs Valley, Dudley, Springville, Graham, Tazewell, Cedar Bluff, Raven, and Richlands in Tazewell County

In New York: Edgewood in Scarsdale; Todd in Briarcliff Manor; Lindsay in Montrose; Katonah School in Katonah; Increase Miller in Goldens Bridge; Oregon Middle in Medford; South Ocean and Saxton Middle in Patchogue; Columbus in Thornwood; Kensico in Valhalla; and Davis in New Rochelle

In Iowa: Westwood, East, Southeast, Terrace, Northeast, and Northwest Schools in Ankeny; Wilkins, Novak, Indian Creek, and Francis Marion in Marion; and Westfield and Bowman Woods in Cedar Rapids

In Michigan: Beechview, Hillside, Longacre, Forest, Eagle, Wooddale, Kenbrook, Gill, and HCC Schools in Farmington Hills; and Ealy, Green, and Doherty in West Bloomfield

In California: Excelsior School in Roseville; Ridgeview and Eureka in Granite Bay; La Entrada, Encinal, and Las Lomitas in Menlo Park; and Corte Madera in Portola Valley

In Nevada: Rex Bell, Bonner, Lummis, Myrtle Tate, May, and Cashman Schools in Las Vegas

In Georgia: Walker and Addison Schools in Marietta; Hickory Flat in Canton; Fair Street in Gainesville; City Park in Dalton; and Holy Innocents in Atlanta

In Connecticut: Holmes and Tokeneke School in Darien

Acknowledgments

Thanks to Kelly Grimm of the Outer Banks History Center; David Kelly; Betty Brown; and Tracy Meeheib of the Library of Congress; Kate Igoe of the National Air and Space Museum; Darrell Collins of the Wright Memorial; Michael Hicklin of the Norfolk Public Library; Nina Wallace; Emily Thomas; and Johnny Moore's granddaughter Karen Brickhouse and his daughter-in-law May Moore.

Witnesses of this flight, besides my brother and myself, were John T. Daniels, W. S. Dough, A. D. Etheridge, from the Kill Devil Life Saving Station; W. C. Brinkley, of Manteo; and Johnny Moore, a boy from Nags Head, North Carolina.

—Orville Wright

I reckon there must be a ton of words written about those fellers Orville and Wilbur Wright. Some of the words are true, some of them are lies, but mostly the words are just left out cause the folks who wrote 'em weren't there when it all happened.

Well, I was there. I was there when Mr. Wilbur and Mr. Orville first came to Kitty Hawk back in 1900. I was there on December 17th, 1903, the day they got that durn flying machine off the ground. And I set it down on paper back then just like it happened.

It's been 50 years now. All the other folks who were there back then are gone now. But I'm still here. I'm the last living witness. I was only a boy then, and I'm an old man now. Soon I'll be gone too and there won't be no witnesses left.

I pulled out my old diaries and scrapbooks to help me remember what happened. You can look at 'em if you like.

Johnny Moore
1950

Contents

Contents

Book 1: 1900
GO FLY A KITE

For some years I have been afflicted with the belief that flight is possible to man. My disease has increased in severity and I feel that it will soon cost me an increased amount of money if not my life.

—Wilbur Wright

January 1, 1900

Today is the first day of a new century! That's something, innit?

To celebrate, mama hands me this book. It says JOHNNY MOORE on the cover, which is my name. I say why would anybody write a book about ME, and mama says it's not about YOU. I say what am I gonna do with some book about ANOTHER Johnny Moore, as I don't go in much for readin' anyway. I told mama if you wanted to get me a present, you might could have got me a new fishin' pole or somethin' I could use. But she says it's a special book and I should open it.

So I open the book and THERE AIN'T NO WORDS ON THE DURN PAGES! Nary a one! I say what good is a book with no words in it? About as useful as a fish hook with no bait.

I reckon I could read this book right fast, not havin' to slow down to read no words. But mama says the trick is I gotta write my OWN words in the pages.

Shucks, who ever heard of a book you put your OWN words into? I never heard of such a thing.

But Mama is a right smart woman. She tells people's fortunes for money, and she knows about things most folks don't know. Like, it was mama who told me if your left hand itches, that means you're gonna get some money. And if you find a cricket in the house, that means it's gonna rain. She knows all the important rules like that.

Mama says if I write in this book every day for a year and fill up the whole book with words, good things will come to me. But I don't believe that for a minute and I tell her I won't do it. So mama says fine, don't write in the durn book for all I care.

That's when I got an idea. I say to mama how about I write in the book every day, but I don't have to go to school no more? She says WHAT???

See, I never DID like school. Last year mean old Miz Hamilton would hit me in the palm with her brass ruler when I misbehaved, which was most of the time. I'm 14 years old now anyhow, and I don't need no more learnin'. Lots of folks who are all grown up don't know how to read near as good as me. Besides, if I don't have to be wastin' time goin to school, I could make more money fishin' and helpin' mama.

Mama thinks it over and thinks it over and thinks it over some more. See, she never went to school when she was little. She taught herself everything. But she wanted ME to get educated, and it means a lot to her that I made it all the way to 7th grade. But finally she says okay, your deal is agreeable to me. But you better write in the book, Johnny, and you better use good grammar cause I don't want you sounding like some dumb cracker.

So if I write in this durn book every day, I don't have to go to school no more. Whoopee!

And look, I filled up nearbout a whole page ALREADY!

January 31, 1900

Okay, so I didn't write in the durn book every day like I told mama I would. But I didn't have nothin' to SAY! What am I s'posed to write about, how I went a-fishin', which is what I do most every day? Mama says YES.

Okay, so I fish and hunt and crab and trap and whittle a little. I sell my catch for money to the dingbatters who come out here in the summer and don't have the sense to catch their own grub. I catch oysters, shad, herring, rock bass, croaker, and bluefish. Ain't much more to say about it. Can't fill up no book with THAT.

But now there's big news to write about. I just heard next season they're startin' up a whole new baseball league! It's gonna be called the American League and there's talk that some-day they'll play against the best team in the National League in a World Serious to see whose better. That's somethin', innit?

I'm afraid my Chicago Orphans might could join up this new league cause they come in 8th place in the National League last year. They're a pretty sorry team, but we ain't got no major league team out here in North Carolina so I gotta pull for SOME-BODY.

I hear The Orphans got this new feller name of Frank Chance who they say is good. Maybe with him, they will have a chance.

Hey, that's a joke! The Orphans have a Chance.

February 2, 1900

Mama read what I wrote in the book and she was powerful sore at me. She says writin' about baseball foolishness wasn't what she had in mind when she gave me the book and why don't I write about important matters? Like what, I says, cause nothin' important ever happens out here on the Outer Banks. She says think of something or you're gonna have to go back to school.

Maybe I won't let mama read the book no more.

March 6, 1900

Happy birthday to ME! THAT'S pretty important, innit? I

was born in the year 1885, which makes me 15 today. If I make it to 50 years, it will be the year 1935. If I make it to 100 years, it will be the year 1985. And if—oh forget it.

Mama don't have much money, but she got me a pair of shoes and an old safety bicycle that one of the surfmen over at the Kitty Hawk Life Saving Station was sellin'. I fixed it up, and it is a dasher. I am gonna ride it everywhere. The shoes I ain't got no use for, as I reckon I like the feel of sand under my feet just fine.

June 20, 1900

Okay, so I didn't write in the book every day. But now something REALLY important happened that even mama will think is important. Mr. Teddy Roosevelt is gonna be runnin' for Vice President with President McKinley who's runnin' for re-election. They're a-goin' against some feller from Nebraska name of William Jennings Bryan. The election will be in November.

I hear that Mr. Roosevelt likes to go a-huntin' like me, so I guess I'm a-pullin' for him and Mr. McKinley to beat the stuffin' outta that Bryan feller.

August 8, 1900

What a HORRIBLE day! It all started when mama wakes me up and says, Johnny, get up. You got to go to Chloe Beasley's birthday party. Chloe Beasley is this little squirt of a girl who lives up the road a piece. She turned 5 years old today. So I say to mama I am 15 why do I have to go to some little GIRLY party? Mama says there ain't many children round here and Chloe will feel all sad if she ain't got enough friends at her party. So mama makes me go and even makes me wear my new shoes, too.

So I go to Chloe's house and who do I find but me and Chloe and her mama and NOBODY ELSE. I felt like crawlin' in a hole and pullin' the hole in after me.

Chloe started in cryin' cause some of her little friends couldn't come to her party. So I tried to cheer her up some with games and piggyback rides and such. She stopped crying. The good thing was Chloe's mama let me take my shoes off, and me and Chloe got to eat the whole birthday cake by ourselves.

September 12, 1900

Okay, so I ain't been writin' in the book much. But heck, the fish don't get caught when I'm wastin' time puttin' words in a durn book. And if I don't catch no fish, I don't make no money. And mama don't make enough money tellin' fortunes by herself, leastways not once the summer is over and all the dingbatters venture back to the mainland.

But I heard tell that somethin' real interestin' happened the other night. 'Bout nine o'clock, they say, this boat come in with this dingbatter from Ohio. This feller come ashore with 3 trunkloads of stuff, a bunch of long wooden rods, spools of wire, and a mess of white cloth. What's he need THAT for?

The guy was all dressed up in a jacket and tie like he was goin' to church or a funeral or somethin'. Nobody round here gets dressed up for no boat ride. I figure this dingbatter must be crazy or somethin'.

Now, I wasn't at the wharf at Kitty Hawk when the feller rolls in. But I know it's the honest truth cause I got it straight from my chum Elijah Baum who saw the whole thing and I know

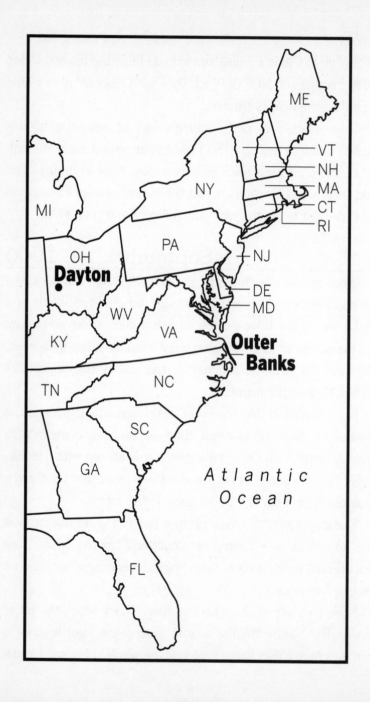

he wouldn't lie. Well not usually. Elijah lives by the water and likes to sail model boats in Kitty Hawk Bay. Me and mama live a whoop and a holler down the beach in Nags Head.

Anyhow, Elijah says this stranger took a whole week to get from Dayton, Ohio, by train, skiff, and who knows what else. He was so tuckered and sore from sleepin' on the deck that he could barely walk. The guy told Elijah he ain't eaten nothin' but jelly for two days.

I say to Elijah why did the guy tote all that junk out here for, and Elijah says wait wait I'm gettin' to that part. I hate it when Elijah does that.

Anyway, Elijah says he took the dingbatter to Captain Bill Tate's house a quarter mile from the wharf. Captain Tate is prettymost the smartest man in Dare County, havin' went to high school and all. He's the postmaster and county commissioner and who knows what else. Captain Tate's wife is named Amanda, but everybody calls her Miz Addie. They got two little gals name of Pauline and Irene.

Elijah says Miz Addie made the dingbatter from Ohio a heap of ham and eggs. He swooped down on 'em like a starvin' hawk and went to sleep for the rest of the day.

Yeah, so what is the guy doin' here I say to Elijah and he says hold my horses and he'll tell me in a minute.

Next mornin', says Elijah, the dingbatter and Captain Tate went to the wharf and used a horse cart to haul the feller's stuff ashore. They was totin' crates and a tent and some pieces of pine lumber that was 16 foot long, in addition to all his other stuff.

What's the dingbatter buildin' I ask, and Elijah STILL won't tell me. He likes to stretch out a story so's you want to hear the

end. Elijah goes on and tells me the dingbatter asked the Tates for a gallon of boiled water every day. That's all he wanted. BOILED WATER! Seems his brother come close to dyin' a few years back from typhoid, so he's feared of bad water. Can't fault him for that. Typhoid can kill a man near quick as a bullet.

The next thing this crazy dingbatter did was order a barrel of gasoline. He had it shipped 50 mile from Elizabeth City. Elijah said the dingbatter's gonna keep the gasoline right in his tent!

What is he, touched, I ask. I know for sure that I ain't goin' anywhere near THAT tent in case it gets blowed up. This dingbatter is surely touched in the head.

Finally, I says to Elijah that if he don't tell me what the guy is buildin', I'm gonna frap him acrost the jaw. Okay, says Elijah. Then he doesn't say nothin' for a while till I'm just about to frap him. Then he says this—the dingbatter is buildin' hisself . . . A FLYIN' MACHINE! Don't that beat all?

Well, I frap Elijah in the jaw anyhow. Here I am wastin' 15 perfectly good minutes of my time just to hear him make up one of his dumb stories. I tell him I got fish to catch. And just to be on the safe side, I take another poke at Elijah.

September 13, 1900

Well, it turns out that Elijah was tellin' the God's honest truth. A crazy dingbatter DID come all the way from Ohio, and he IS buildin' a flying machine. Leastways, that's what everyone's sayin' at the general store. It's just about the most excitin' thing to happen round here since Blackbeard the Pirate hisself washed up on these shores, and that was nearbout 2 hunnerd years ago.

So I says to myself, why would a feller come all the way from Ohio to the Outer Banks of North Carolina? Why don't he just build his flyin' machine in Ohio?

It ain't exactly paradise here on the Banks. We're just a 2 hunnerd mile spit of sand 'tween the Atlantic Ocean and Albemarle Sound, bent like an elbow. We ain't got nothin' here that a dingbatter like him would want, near as I can tell.

You can't hardly grow no crops here. Folks try to grow corn and beans in the sand. But the only thing that grows good here are bedbugs, wood ticks, and skeeters.

Most folks don't want to come here cause the weather ain't very tolerable. There's no point in ever combin' your hair cause we got so much wind it just blows your hair everywhichways. 'Specially in the winter. It sounds like thunder. The sand blows

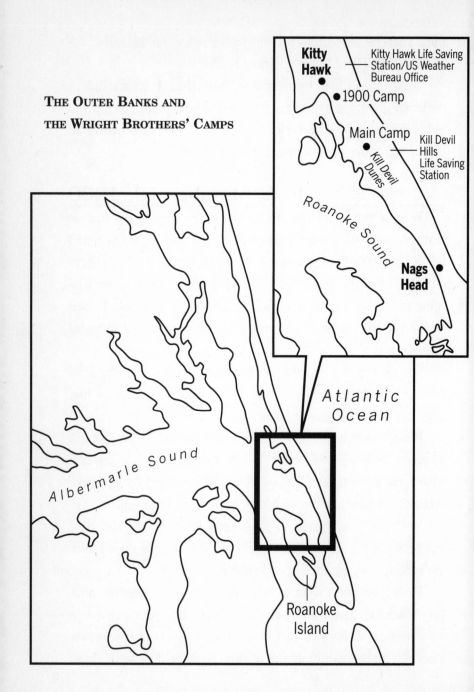

THE OUTER BANKS AND THE WRIGHT BROTHERS' CAMPS

so hard it can bury a house. You can close your eyes, but the sand gets everywhere else. Even in your underclothes. You get used to it, like most everything else, I spose. I ain't never been to Ohio, but I reckon if I went there, I'd stay there.

The only town we got, 'cept for Nags Head, is Kitty Hawk, which ain't hardly much of a town anyhow. They got about 20 houses, some stores, a church, and a school with one teacher for everybody, no matter how old you are.

'Tween Kitty Hawk and Nags Head it's flatter than a runned-over ground hog for nearbout 5 miles, 'cept for some sand dunes near Kitty Hawk and woods on the side. Every so often you can see the top branches of trees stickin' out of the sand. They was buried years ago. Other than that, there's just a lot of nothin'.

The only good thing we DO got here is fishin' and huntin'. I fish in the spring and summer, and hunt in the fall. The woods are filled with wild game. When you look in the water, you can see dozens of fish swimmin' about, just waitin' to be caught. You look up in the sky and you can see eagles, buzzards, seagulls, redbirds, wrens, sparrows, ospreys, mockingbirds, you name it.

But from what I hear, this dingbatter from Ohio don't look like no hunter and he don't look like no fisherman neither.

That's when I figured it out. The dingbatter must be a spy.

I know all about spies. I read in some book about spies stealin' secrets and sellin' 'em to the enemy and such. I don't know what secrets we have round here, but we must have some durn good ones or this dingbatter wouldn't be comin' here tryin' to steal 'em.

He GOT to be a spy. Prob'bly thinks we're a bunch of dumb

country crackers he can spy on and take our secrets back to Ohio.

Well shucks, I'll go him one better. I'm gonna spy on HIM. That will learn him.

September 14, 1900

I resolved to spy on the dingbatter from a distance for a spell. So I rode my bicycle over near the Tate house where this dingbatter was a-stayin'. There was a pile of firewood about a hunnerd foot from Captain Tate's front porch, perfect for spyin' behind. If some feller was buildin' a flyin' machine, I wanted to see it fly.

For a long time not a soul come out of the Tate house. I spied the long pieces of lumber under a canvas shelter on the front lawn, though. Something was up. Captain Tate is a lot of things, but he ain't no builder. After 30 minutes or so of waitin' I was fixin' to venture home when this feller come out of the house. I got a good look at him.

He looked like a bird, is the best I can describe. He was a tall, bony feller, nearbout 6 foot with no hair on his head 'cept for some which wrapped round the side and back. He was walkin' round lookin' at his wood and stuff. I thought I saw him lookin' in my direction, so I took off.

September 15, 1900

I went back for another peek at the dingbatter and his machine. This time I see him bright and early, still all dressed up like he was fixin' to go to church, but he was a-sawin' on wood. After a spell Captain Tate come over and lended him a hand. Then Miz Addie come out on the front porch a-wheelin' her sewin' machine.

Soon Miz Addie was pumpin' on the foot pedal and sewin' some long white cloth, while Captain Tate was hammerin' and the dingbatter was sawin'. The three of 'em was busier than a bee in a tar barrel.

I'll say one thing, it didn't look like they was buildin' no flyin' machine. Looked more like a long dinner table or some such thing, if you ask me. I will do further spyin' tomorrow to get at the truth.

September 16, 1900

Mama is powerful happy with what I wrote in this book so far. She said, "Johnny, you keep this up and you won't have to go to school ever again." That sounded good to me. Mama did holler at me about my spelling and grammar, and I told her I'd try to write more better. Mama says I should see how close I can get to the dingbatter so I might could write down what he says.

When I went back to the Tate house, the dingbatter and his stuff was gone. I thought he mighta gone back to Ohio, but then I spied a tent about a half mile down the beach. The dingbatter must have toted his stuff out there. He tied the tent to one of the only trees round, so it won't blow away, I reckon.

I walked my bicycle over near there, all casual, like I was huntin' for horseshoe crabs in the sand. Then suddenly the dingbatter come out of the tent. It was too late to make a run for it or he woulda knowed I was a-spyin' on him.

As he come over to me I could see he got big ears stickin' out and a sharp nose like a hawk. Closer still and he's got this Adams apple juttin' out and these gray blue eyes borin' in on me. It was almost frightful.

"Young man!" the dingbatter yells to me. "What's your name, son?"

He talked all proper, like a preacher or Englishman or something. I tell him my name is Johnny Moore from Nags Head and he says his name is Wilbur Wright and then he spelled it for me, W-R-I-G-H-T.

"Are you a spy?" I ask, and he says, "No, but I thought YOU were. I've seen you watching me these past few days."

"I was a-huntin' for seashells," I say, and I glance up to see if he was buyin' it. I weren't sure, and seein' as how I weren't totin' no seashells, I figured I best change the subject fast. "Folks say you're buildin' a flyin' machine," I say.

"It's a kite," says Mr. Wilbur. "If it flies successfully, I will try to lie on it and glide it. And if I can figure out how to control it, I may build a powered flying machine at some point. Did you come around to witness my experiments?"

"Nope," I says. "I just wanted to see if your tent blew away yet."

It is my belief that flight is possible, and while I am taking up the investigation for pleasure rather than profit, I think there is a slight possibility of achieving fame and fortune from it.

—Wilbur Wright, in a letter to his father, September 3, 1900

Now, this Mr. Wilbur and I both know nobody NEVER built a flyin' machine afore. Leastways, nobody ever built one that FLEW. Sure, I memorized there was this feller name of James Gatling who lived in Murfreesboro, nearbout 85 mile from here. James built this flying machine a few years back. People still talk about it. They called it Old Turkey Buzzard.

Gatling chucked his machine off a roof one day and it fell on a tree, which don't hardly count for flyin'. That weren't likely to happen here, though, cause we ain't got many trees.

I pretended the dingbatter was perfectly normal, like he was buildin' a boat or something useful instead of somethin' crazy like a flyin' machine.

"No foolin'?" says I. "Are you a scientist?"

"No," says he. "I operate a bicycle shop with my brother in Dayton, Ohio." He tells me that after the summer is over, not many folks in Ohio buy bicycles, so he's got time to fool round with flyin' machines and such.

As he's talkin' I'm thinkin' in my head, A BICYCLE

SHOP? He runs a bicycle shop, and this dingbatter thinks he's gonna build a FLYIN' MACHINE? He IS touched. But I don't say that.

"You musta gone to some fancy college, eh?" I says.

"The truth be told, I never even graduated from high school."

Now I'm SURE the feller is touched. But again, I don't say it.

"Why you wanna build a flyin' machine?" I ask. "You wanna be rich and famous?"

"No," he says. "There are many practical uses for a flying machine. It could be used for the delivery of mail, for instance. Or perhaps someday people will fly to get somewhere instead of taking a train or boat or automobile. But mostly, I just want to see if it can be done."

"Uh-huh."

Then he sits down on the sand and almost half closes his eyes like he's thinkin' of the far away.

"You see, one day when I was 11-years old and my brother was 7, our father brought home a present for us. He pulled something out of his pocket and it flew out of his hand. It was a toy flying machine made from paper, bamboo, cork, and rubber bands. We called it The Bat. Ever since then, I have been fascinated by the idea of human flight."

This feller was somethin'. I swear I never heard a grown man go on so long without sayin' one cuss word.

"Flight is one of mankind's most vexing problems," he says, "and I believe it can be solved. Johnny, did you ever want to do something nobody has ever done in the history of the world? Did you ever want to do something people have dreamed of for thousands of years? Did you ever want to solve a problem that has stumped mankind for centuries?"

"Never thought about it afore," says I. "I reckon catchin' fish is good enough for me."

He says nothin' and looks round like he oughta be gettin' back to work. "Say, shouldn't you be in school?" he says.

"Well, maybe I should be, but I ain't. Don't need no schoolin' to fish and hunt."

Mr. Wilbur asks if I would sell him some fish, and I say I ain't got no fish to sell, and he says what kind of a fisherman has no fish to sell and I say the kind of fisherman who done sold all his fish already and ain't caught more yet.

Then he asked where my mama was at, and I told him my mama is in Nags Head tellin' fortunes and she gets a whole 25 cents for every fortune she tells, which is good money, considerin' she only tells people what they wanna hear anyhow. Then he asked where my daddy is at, and I tell him I ain't got no daddy cause my daddy, King Solomon Moore, passed this life when I was little and went to a better world.

He looked discomfortable, and I reckon he was lookin' to change the subject, cause the next thing he asked me had nothin' to do with my mama or daddy. He asked me why they call the Outer Banks The Graveyard of the Atlantic. I tell him it's cause ships can't seem to help but disappear round here.

See, not long after the Spanish explorers washed up at Nags Head Woods round the year 1500 something, this Sir Walter Raleigh feller started up a colony right nearby on Roanoke Island. Turns out the whole lot of 'em disappeared without a trace and now they call it The Lost Colony.

Maybe it was pirates who killed 'em, cause they come next. This feller named Edward Teach called hisself Blackbeard and lived down in Ocracoke. He did a lot of lootin' and killin' till 1700 something, when they chopped his head off and hung it from a ship. Folks say his headless body swum round the ship 3 times afore it finally went under. Sounds like a tall tale, but you never know.

Anyway, by Blackbeard's day they was callin' these parts Chickahauk. Coulda been an old Indian word or a way of sayin' chicken hawk, or whatever. A hunnerd years later folks were callin' it Kitty Hawk.

Most families lived here for 2 hunnerd years or more and never mingled much with dingbatters. Ain't nothin' over on the mainland we ain't got right here, so there ain't no reason to venture there. ISN'T, I mean. Mama told me I'm s'posed to write ISN'T 'stead of AIN'T. But it just don't come natural.

Most folks I know are descended from colonists, pirates, spies, or shipwrecked castaways who crawled ashore and settled on the beaches. Mama says I prob'bly got some pirate blood in me and that's why I'm so rambunctious, whatever that means.

Mr. Wilbur listens to everything I say, starin' at me with those scary blue eyes and thin lips. He tells me he ain't a spy and he ain't a pirate and he ain't a castaway. He just come here to fly kites.

"They got some law against flyin' kites in Ohio?" I ask.

"I need steady winds to provide lift, and sand for soft landings. I can't get that in Ohio."

Well, if he come here for wind and sand, we got 'em. That's about all we got, but we got plenty.

"Wind, sand, and solitude," he says. "I would prefer to conduct my experiments in private."

I tell Mr. Wilbur that if he wants, I could ask my mama to tell his fortune and find out if his flyin' machine is gonna fly or not. He says that would be just fine, and if I ever want to come round his campsite again, I don't have to sneak over. I can just come by and I'd be welcome. He was a strange looking man, but decent enough.

September 17, 1900

I come home and see that squirt Chloe Beasley crying like she does. I ask what's wrong, and she sobs, "Your little calf died." Sure enough, I get home and our calf is dead. Mama is crying too. She told me she went out to milk the cow and she found the calf layin' there dead for no reason. It was just a baby.

Even sadder than mama was the calf's mama. She wouldn't come in to give no milk, and mama says if a cow don't give no milk she's gonna die too. The mama cow was hidin' out in the field and wouldn't come in. We had to do somethin'.

So I come up with an idea. Me and mama skinned the dead calf and stuffed it with straw so it would look alive. When we was done and sewed her up, you couldn't hardly tell she was dead. We propped her up against the fence and called her mama. Sure enough, the cow takes one look at her calf and comes in for milkin'.

Fooled her good! Chloe and mama cheered up a whit, even though Chloe said stuffing a dead calf was disgustin'. But mama said she was proud of me for usin' my engine newity, whatever that is.

September 19, 1900

I rode my bicycle over to Kitty Hawk, which is no easy trick unless you stick close to the water where the beach sand is packed down good and hard. Mr. Wilbur was up early, workin' on his contraption. He told me he wants to have the thing finished by the time his brother arrives in a few days.

I told him about the calf dyin' and how we stuffed it with straw to fool its mama. He said it was most interestin', and things like that don't go on much where he lives in Dayton, Ohio.

"So what did your mother say?" he says, puttin' down his hammer for a whit.

"'Bout what?"

"You told me your mother tells fortunes and you were going to ask her if my flying machine would fly," he reminds me.

"You don't wanna know what mama said, Mr. Wilbur."

"Sure I do."

"Mama says she believes in a good God, a bad Devil, and a hot Hell. And she don't reckon that the Lord intended people should fly. If he did, we woulda been born with wings. That's what she said."

Mr. Wilbur didn't look sore or nothin'. He just says, "People weren't born with WHEELS either. Perhaps you shouldn't be riding your bicycle."

He had me there, and Mr. Wilbur went back to his hammerin'. He ain't much for conversation and I said to him, "You ain't much for conversation, are you?"

"No," was all he said, and I was glad he said that much.

I walk round the machine, lookin' at it. It looked like it was just nearbout done. Finally I say, "Where is the engine?"

"There is no engine, Johnny."

"Well, how you expect to get off the durn ground without an engine?"

Mr. Wilbur put the hammer down. "The problem is not getting off the ground," he says. "The problem is what to do once you get off the ground."

He seen that I didn't understand so he tried to explain hisself better. Mr. Wilbur said a flyin' machine needs three things to fly. First, it needs wings to lift it in the air, and he's got that. Second, it needs to move the wings forward fast enough to heist up, and he reckons he can do that by runnin' the machine down the side of a sand dune. Third, it needs a way to control the thing once it's in the air.

That's the tough part, he says. And that's the part other fellers who tried to fly didn't think of. They got themselves big engines first and tried to use brute strength to heist themselves up. That might could get you off the ground for a second or two, says Mr. Wilbur, but that's all. It ain't real flyin'.

The problem is you can't learn to control the durn thing if you can't get it up in the air, and you can't get it up in the air if you can't control the durn thing.

A pack of buzzards was passin' overhead, and Mr. Wilbur ran inside the tent to get binoculars.

"Look!" he says, handin' 'em to me. "See how those birds turn in flight?"

I looked through the binoculars and seen the birds, but didn't see no more'n that.

"Look at the tips of their wings," says Mr. Wilbur. "See the way the buzzard bends the end of one wing down slightly to make it rise, and then it bends the end of the other wing up to make it drop? That is how I hope to control our flying machine."

We could not understand what it was about a bird that would enable it to fly that could not be built on a larger scale for a man. If a bird could glide through the air without using any muscular effort, why couldn't a man?

—**Wilbur Wright, 1899**

"Why can't we just flap our arms like birds?" I ask as I spy the buzzards through the glass.

"Birds have tremendous strength for their weight," says Mr. Wilbur. "A man would need fifty times his strength to flap his arms and fly."

I look through the binoculars again, but the buzzards flew outta range, so I couldn't see 'em no more. "If you want," I says, "I could shoot one of them buzzards out of the sky for you to peer at it up close."

"I didn't come here to shoot birds," Mr. Wilbur says. "I came to emulate them."

I ain't never heard of no big word like EMULATE, but it sounded like some new way to kill birds and cook 'em. Maybe emulatin' is pokin' a sharp stick through 'em or fryin' 'em. I didn't say nothin' in case I was wrong.

Mr. Wilbur went into his tent again and come out with a thin cardboard box about the size of a man's arm. He takes one end in each hand.

"I call it wing warping," he says, twistin' the ends of the box in diffr'nt directions. "I conducted some tests back in Ohio, and I believe wing warping is the key to controlling human flight, just as it is for bird flight. What do you think, Johnny?"

"I think your BRAIN is warped, is what I think."

"Ah, you may be right," he says, tossin' aside the box. "Learning to fly by watching birds may very well be like learning magic from a magician. Neither desires to reveal their secrets."

September 28, 1900

Friday. Went over to Kitty Hawk to bring Mr. Wilbur some fish I caught. His brother, Orville, showed up presently with his suitcase, another tent, and as much coffee, tea, and sugar as a man could tote with him from Ohio.

Mr. Orville didn't look nothin' like Mr. Wilbur. He was a whit shorter, a whit stockier, and he had thick, curly brown hair and a reddish mustache. He was more talkative and quicker to throw you a smile, too.

When I told him I don't go to school no more, Mr. Orville told me that when he was in 6th grade, he got in trouble and the teacher told him not to come back to school without a parent.

"So what'd you do?" I ask.

"I didn't go back to school!" he says. "I had to pass a test to get into 7th grade."

Mr. Orville told me he was 29, four years younger than his brother. Looked to me like Mr. Wilbur was the boss and Mr.

Orville was his helper. But Mr. Wilbur DID tell his brother he was sorry the glider weren't finished by the time Orv showed up.

That's what he calls him. Mr. Wilbur calls Mr. Orville ORV and Mr. Orville calls Mr. Wilbur WILL. Neither of 'em seems highfalutin', like some dingbatters.

The two commenced to workin' on the contraption together, and 'stead of standin' round, I pitched in too. They didn't crack jokes and tell stories like most fellers do when they're workin'. They didn't say much of anything. I could be standin' right next to 'em, and they wouldn't even notice me. Like I wasn't there. They would just be thinkin' about the wood or the nail or the screwdriver, I guess.

They didn't talk much, but every now and again they would suddenly begin to whistle. Strangest thing. They'd commence to whistlin' the exact similar tune at the exact similar time. Like they planned it or something.

When the sun got low in the sky, they knocked off work and Mr. Orville cooked up the mess of fish I brung, plus a batch of griddle cakes. Mr. Orville is a powerful good cook.

They invited me for supper as long as my mama didn't mind, and I say sometimes I stay out all night and mama don't mind. After we ate, I showed 'em how to wash dishes in the sand. Things don't get very dirty round here, on account of we ain't got no dirt, just sand.

After we cleaned up, the sun goes down behind the clouds and lights 'em up in gold, deep blue, and orange. Mr. Wilbur and Mr. Orville stared up at the sky like they never seen a sunset before. Maybe the sun don't set in Ohio.

When it got dark, we watched the moon come and light up the sand. There was so many stars, you couldn't count. Mr. Orville fished a mandolin out of his things and played quiet and slow. The mockingbirds nearby sang harmony. After a whit we all three lay down on our backs in the sand and stared up at the heavens.

The brothers got to talkin' about flyin', which is what they seem to think about and talk about most all the time.

"You know, I believe a successful flying machine could put an end to warfare forever," says Mr. Orville.

"How do you figure that?" I ask.

"Imagine if a government could observe every movement of its enemy by aeroplane," says Mr. Wilbur. "There could be no surprise attacks. Neither side could get the advantage. No government would risk starting a war."

Seemed to me that some folks just naturally hate each other, and they're gonna fight whether they got sticks, swords, guns, or flyin' machines. But I didn't say nothin' so they wouldn't think me dumb.

For all I know, Mr. Wilbur and Mr. Orville went on talkin' about flyin' machines all night, but I didn't hear it all cause I fell asleep right there on the sand.

I reckon Mr. Wilbur and Mr. Orville ain't spies after all. But I STILL reckon they're crazy.

September 30, 1900

The glider is finished. It's a pretty bird, more than 17 foot wide and 52 pound. The top and bottom wings are covered by the cloth Miz Addie sewed, and they're connected by upright posts called struts. They got wires crisscrossin' the struts so the wings can be warped. It ain't got no tail or nothin'. Mr. Wilbur calls the thing in the front that controls up and down an "elevator."

He told me he spent a heap of jack buildin' the thing. 15 whole dollars.

When the last screw was turned, Mr. Wilbur gets out this big picture-takin' machine that says KORONA-V on it. I seen photographs afore, but I ain't never seen a real camera. Mr. Wilbur snapped a photograph of the aeroplane. He calls it a GLIDER on account it ain't got no engine. He says they'll fly her as a kite tomorrow.

October 1, 1900

The wind weren't strong enough, so it was unfittin' for flyin' today. Mr. Wilbur says he needs a steady wind of 15 or 20 mile per hour to lift the glider up. Captain Tate come round to see if he could help out, but there weren't nothin' for him to do. The Captain don't like everyone, but he seems to take a shine to

Mr. Wilbur and Mr. Orville, cause he comes round from time to time just to talk. I reckon it's cause he has two daughters and wishes he had a son. He treats Mr. Wilbur and Mr. Orville like they was his boys.

October 2, 1900

A hard wind was blowin' from the north, close to 30 mile per hour. Too dangerous to fly. When I got to their camp, Mr. Orville was runnin' up and down the beach flappin' his arms like a bird. Like I said, he and his brother must be touched.

They got their camp set up nice with the tent and all. They ain't got no privy, so they got to use the woods. They ain't got no water, either, so they bathe at the Tates' house.

October 3, 1900

Wednesday. One day the wind blows 10 mile per hour, the next day it blows 60. I venture out to the Wright camp every day, and every day there's somethin' not right with the wind. Mr. Wilbur and Mr. Orville keep makin' more tests and measurements. I went a-fishin'. Don't think they will EVER fly.

October 4, 1900

Finally Mr. Wilbur says it looks like fittin' flyin' weather. A steady wind was blowin' from the northeast. Captain Tate hitched up his horse Don Keyhoaty to a wagon, and we all toted the glider 4 miles down the beach to Kill Devil Hills.

They call it Kill Devil cause in the old days sailors said it would kill the devil to navigate this part of the Banks. There are three big dunes out there. Big Hill is a hunnerd foot high. Little

Hill is 30 foot. West Hill is 60 foot. Me and Captain Tate and the Wrights toted the glider up the side of Big Hill.

I was hopin' they'd chuck the glider off the dune so I could watch it glide down, but nothin' doin'. Mr. Wilbur says they got to fly it as a kite first for practice. I never seen no kite that big and heavy, and I reckoned it wouldn't work.

They tied two ropes to it, with Mr. Orville and Captain Tate each holdin' one. Then we all heisted it up for the wind to catch it, and sure enough, the thing lifted!

"Look at that!" I hollered. "It's flyin'!"

I was hopin' they'd let out all the rope and see how high the thing would go, but nothin' doin'. Mr. Wilbur only let 'em fly it 5 or 10 foot up. When the kite was steady in the wind, he grabbed a rope that warped the wings and, sure enough, was able to make the thing dip and dive anywhichway he wanted.

Then he grabbed his picture takin' machine and took some snaps. After every picture he wrote down all the particulars in this notebook he toted with him everywhere.

"Can I get a ride?" I say after we been kite-flyin' for a whit. But Mr. Wilbur says it's too dangerous for me cause it ain't perfected yet.

Instead he clum in the thing hisself and says he's gonna give it a try. Mr. Orville and Captain Tate each held a wingtip as Mr. Wilbur lay down in the middle of the lower wing, belly buster style. He put his feet on a T-shaped bar that worked the wing warpin'. Then he switched his cap round so the beak pointed to the back and wouldn't fall off. Then he put his hands on the forward elevator control.

"Go!" says he.

Captain Tate and Mr. Orville commenced to run into the wind and down the side of the dune. Presently the kite begun to heist up, and the men begun lettin' out the rope slowly.

I let out a whoop. "Lookit that!" I hollered. "Shucks, you're flyin', Mr. Wilbur!"

The kite was no more'n 15 foot up when it begun to dink up and down everywhichways like a drunk buzzard. Mr. Wilbur was workin' the elevator, but evertime he moved it, the kite would dart up or down instead of flyin' straight like he was tryin' to make it do.

"Let me down!" he hollers, so they do.

After they rassle the thing to the sand, we all run over to see if Mr. Wilbur is okay.

"Why did you stop, Will?" Mr. Orville says.

Mr. Wilbur was scared. I could see it in his eyes. He looked like he seen a ghost.

"I promised Pop I'd take care of myself," says he as he clum out of the machine.

Before trying to rise to any dangerous height a man ought to know that in an emergency his mind and muscles will work by instinct rather than by conscious effort. There is no time to think.

—Wilbur Wright

October 5, 1900

Mr. Wilbur musta been so mommicked from flyin' yesterday that he didn't want no part of it no more. 'Stead of gettin' back in the machine hisself, he and his brother was fillin' burlap bags with sand and strappin' 'em to the glider when I showed up on my bicycle. I asked what they was up to, and they say they are conductin' tests.

The surfmen at the Kitty Hawk Life Saving Station had lended 'em an anemometer, which is a thingamabobber that measures the fastness of wind. They had rigged up a fish scale so they could measure air resistance, whatever that is. Then they flew the thing as a kite and wrote down a bunch of numbers in Mr. Wilbur's notebook.

With 60 pound of sand the thing lifted up finely, and Mr. Wilbur was lookin' to add weight, but there weren't room for more sand.

"I reckon I can be a weight!" I says. I'd been a-beggin' for a ride from the start, but so far nothin' doin'.

"How much do you weigh, Johnny?" Mr. Orville asks.

"Nearbout 90 pound," say I.

Mr. Wilbur looks at Mr. Orville, and Mr. Orville looks at Mr. Wilbur, like they was thinkin' things over and might give me a ride 'gainst their better judgment. I put on my best puppy-dog face, and they say well, okay.

I clum on with a whoop, and Mr. Wilbur says not to touch the controls no matter what, but just lie there. Fine by me. Didn't know how to work no controls anyhow.

"Go ahead," I says, "chuck her off the dune! I'll land her prettier than a hawk swoopin' on a sunfish."

Mr. Wilbur and Mr. Orville grab the wingtips and start a-runnin'. Then the wind catches me, and they let go. I WAS FLYIN'!

But I weren't goin' nowheres. I was just stayin' in one place, about 10 foot off the sand. I look down and see both Wrights holdin' the ropes.

"Higher!" I holler. "Let them ropes free!"

But nothin' doin'. They pulled me down after a whit. My heart was beatin' like a drum, but I wanted to go again. Mr. Wilbur said the glider weren't perfected, and he was afraid my mama would be ornery if I busted up my head or something.

October 6, 1900

Saturday. Rain and hard winds. No tests. So I went home. That squirt Chloe Beasley sees me and says where you been all mornin'? I say none of your business. That's all I need, some little girl pokin' fun at me cause I been foolin' round with some crazy dingbatters. Chloe asked me if I want to play, and I said I don't play with toys. She looked like she was gonna cry, and I felt bad for saying it.

October 7, 1900

Sunday. I come by the Wright camp hopin' for another ride, but they tell me there won't be no flyin' today. I ask why not, and they say they promised their pa back in Ohio that they won't never fly on a Sunday. Their pa is a bishop, and Sunday is s'posed to be a day of rest. I tell 'em their pa won't know if they fly or don't fly, but that don't make no differnce to them. So I left.

October 9, 1900

Tuesday. Went to the Wright camp. The wind was a-blowin' 36 miles per hour, which is too hard for flyin'. So I left and went a-fishin'. I reckon that's one good thing about fish. They don't care how hard the winds blow, cause they live under water.

October 10, 1900

Wednesday. No sign of Mr. Wilbur or Mr. Orville anywheres. I reckoned they give up and went back to Ohio. Then I seen a little tower over at Lookout Hill, just south of the village at the edge of the dunes. The tower wasn't there yesterday, I was sure of that. I rode my bicycle over.

Turned out the Wrights built a wooden derrick with a pulley on it. Mr. Wilbur says he's fixin' to attatch the glider to the pulley and fly it from the derrick. That way, he can hover in the air for long spells and get practice controllin' the contraption.

The wind was nearbout 30 mile per hour, 'cordin' to the anemometer thingy. Mr. Orville attatched the rope to the glider, and the two of 'em heisted it up into the wind. It lifted up maybe 20 foot and woulda went higher 'cept for the rope holdin' it to the derrick.

The durn machine woulda up and flew away, it was pullin' so hard. I was hopin' they'd cut the rope and let 'er fly, but nothin' doin'. Mr. Orville said it would crash and they'd have to rebuild it.

Well, they shoulda took my advice, cause it crashed anyhow. The wind quit suddenly, and the glider darted for the sand. It hit elevator first, crushin' it. Then a hard wind sneaked up, flipped it over, and throwed it 20 foot down the beach. By the time we got to the glider, the right side was smashed in, some struts were busted, and the wires were snapped. It was a wreck.

"This machine needs a doctor pretty badly," Mr. Orville says as they pick up the pieces.

"Maybe we should go home," says Mr. Wilbur, all full of gloom. He can be a gloomy Gus sometimes.

Well, I couldn't take it no more! If I had builded MY own glider and it cracked up like that, I'd a been cussin' a blue streak.

"How come you two fellers never cuss?" I says. "I never met a man that didn't cuss."

"Cussing is for people who lack a vocabulary," says Mr. Wilbur.

I didn't know what a VOCABULARY was, but I reckon I must not have one, cause I cuss all the time. But I won't cuss round Mr. Wilbur and Mr. Orville cause they are so proper.

After the crack up Mr. Wilbur and Mr. Orville decided to change the name of Lookout Hill. Now they call it The Hill of the Wreck.

There are two ways to learn how to ride a wild horse. The first way is to get on him. The second way is to watch him from a distance. It is certainly safer to choose the second option. But the first option will make a better rider. It's the same with flying. If you want to be safe, you can sit on a fence and watch the birds. But if you want to fly, you have to get on your machine and figure out how to make it work.

—Wilbur Wright

October 15, 1900

Turns out the glider weren't as busted up as they thought. The Wrights spent Friday and Saturday a-diggin' pieces of the glider outta the sand and puttin' it back together. Mr. Wilbur said he would never use a derrick again, and he'll just have to fly the thing off the dune. Well, I coulda told him THAT.

On Sunday (the day of rest) I invited Mr. Wilbur and Mr. Orville a-huntin'. They didn't want to at first but then agreed. We chased buzzards and bald eagles for a spell, and I guess they changed their minds about emulatin' birds, cause Mr. Orville shot a chicken hawk outta the sky with my shotgun like he'd been a-shootin' his whole life.

We scooped the bird up and spread her out on the sand. Mr. Wilbur measured the wingspan to 5 foot. He and Mr. Orville examined it everywhichway. Then we cooked it up and ate it.

October 18, 1900

We brung the glider over to Kill Devil Hill on Captain Tate's horse cart. Mr. Wilbur looked all serious, even more than usual, like he was a-goin' to a funeral. I reckon he wanted to fly, but then again, he was afraid after what happened last time.

Mr. Wilbur clum in the glider and lay down. Captain Tate and Mr. Orville each grub aholt a wingtip and run it down the hill and let go.

The wind took it and carried the thing a while, almost down to the bottom, a few foot off the sand the whole way. It was glidin' maybe 5 seconds. Me and Captain Tate run down and see it whack gentle into the side of the hill and stop. When we get to the bottom, Mr. Wilbur was still spittin' out sand.

"It feels like flying!" he says, a smile on his face for one of the first times I remember. "It's like nothing I've ever experienced. Floating, gliding, such a feeling of freedom!"

We toted the glider back up the hill, which was no fun at all. Mr. Wilbur wanted to try it again and again, so we had to keep totin' it up the hill over and over. I could of swore each time they put more weight on it. Mr. Wilbur did all the flyin'. Mr. Orville didn't never even ask for a turn.

By noontime I was so tuckered I reckoned I might could drop dead right in the sand and they would have to bury me there. But Mr. Wilbur wanted one more glide. So we tote the thing up again and chuck it off the hill. It sailed way furthest than all the other times. Mr. Orville measured it out at 4 hunnerd feet and 15 seconds in the air.

Mr. Wilbur says let's quit while we're ahead and break for lunch. I was fine by that!

While we were eating, they talked it all over, quiet and serious. I didn't get it all, but I got this much. Mr. Wilbur ain't happy with the wings and he ain't happy with the up and down control. He says the wings don't give hardly no lift till you get up to 25 mile per hour or so, and it's too confusin' to work the wing warpin' and the elevator at the same time.

Mr. Orville, who is always sunnier, says the wing warpin' 'pears to be the way to go for turns, and puttin' the elevator up in front makes it near impossible to go into a nosedive, which would surely kill the pilot in a wreck.

"At least you didn't get your brains dashed out," Mr. Orville says, tryin' to cheer his brother up. "And we've certainly had a nice vacation."

But nothin' Mr. Orville said cheered Mr. Wilbur up.

"Can I have a ride?" I says when I can get a word in edge-wise.

"Not now, Johnny," Mr. Wilbur tells me. "It's not perfected yet. Maybe next year."

Next YEAR? That's when they broke the news to me. They're gonna pack up camp and venture back home to Ohio.

October 23, 1900

I rode over to Kitty Hawk to see Mr. Wilbur and Mr. Orville off. Captain Tate was already there to take 'em to the wharf.

Just afore they left for the trip across Albemarle Sound, they decided to give the glider one more go for the heck of it. We all carried it up to the top of Little Hill and chucked it off. The thing sailed a ways and skimmed the sand finely to stop. Mr. Wilbur reckoned that since they built the thing, it spent a grand total of two whole minutes in the air.

"You takin' the glider home with you?" Captain Tate asks, and they say no. They learned heaps from the machine, but it ain't worth nothin' now. They're gonna build a NEW flyin' machine over the winter and come back next year to test it.

They shoveled a heap of sand on the glider so it wouldn't blow away and we said our goodbyes.

I gotta admit, I'm sorry to see Mr. Wilbur and Mr. Orville go. But I still reckon those dingbatters was touched in the head.

November 8, 1900

Well, guess what? President McKinley and Mr. Roosevelt won the election on Tuesday! And you know what else? I

FILLED ALL THE PAGES IN THIS DURN BOOK! That's something, innit?

So Mama bought me a NEW book with no words in it 'cept the title on the cover that says 1901. She said my spelling and grammar are still a mess, but I did a good job writing and I don't have to go to school so long as I fill this new book with words. That should be no bother, as I filled the first book almost without even tryin'. Mama said she will buy me a new book with no words in it every year until I'm grown up and can buy my own durn books.

She also bought me this brand new book with words already in it called The Wonderful Wizard of Oz. I peeked in the pages, and this is the strangest book I ever did read. Kind of interestin', though.

Book 2: 1901
RACE FOR THE SKY

We saw that the calculations upon which
all flying-machines had been based were
unreliable, and that all were simply
groping in the dark.

—Orville and Wilbur Wright

January 1, 1901

Happy new year! I got no time to write cause I got to finish fixin' my boat and mendin' all the nets or I won't be catchin' many fish this year. I'll write in this book in a couple of days for sure.

March 6, 1901

Well, happy birthday to ME! I turned 16, so I reckon I'm now a man. Mama still don't like that I say AIN'T too much, but I have smarted up heaps since last year, and as long as I write in this book, I will never have to go back to school no more. Hooray for THAT.

So much has went on since last year, and I ain't had no time to write about it. That Queen Victoria lady passed on. She was the queen of England or some such place. I don't know. The newspaper says some Italian feller by the name of Macaroni figured out a way to send signals by radio waves, with no wires or nothin'. I for one will believe that when I see it. And everybody's talkin' about this new music they call ragtime. I ain't heard it yet cause mama says we ain't got no money to waste on no phonograph.

Baseball season is startin' up soon, and this new American League is for real. They got lots of teams—Boston, Philadelphia, Milwaukee, Detroit, Washington, Cleveland, Baltimore. They even got a team in Chicago called The White Stockings. But they won't play against my Chicago Orphans because the Orphans are in the other league, the National League. Word is maybe next year they'll play a World Serious to see which team is the best of both leagues. I'll believe THAT when I see it too.

Mama made me invite that squirt Chloe Beasley over for birthday cake. I say why, and she says Chloe invited me to HER birthday last year so I gotta invite her to MINE. It was okay, though, cause her mama gave me a new pocket knife for whittlin'. She says I'm the only one who can make Chloe laugh, and that's why she got me the nice present.

July 9, 1901

I thought I seen the last of them crazy Wright dingbatters back in October. But the rumor is that a heap of flyin' machine parts showed up at the Kitty Hawk wharf the other day. Wood, cloth, tools, supplies, and such. I got a feelin' who belongs to it. Who else would be sendin' that stuff here?

July 10, 1901

We DO get some weather in these parts. And last night we got just about as much weather as we could stand. First them black clouds roll in, and you just know what's a-comin'. Time to board up the windows good.

Then come the hard winds. It is so powerful you can't hardly walk if you try. If you walk AGAINST the wind, you gotta just about crawl on your hands and knees to get anywheres. And if you walk AWAY from the wind, it nearbout picks you up and flings you up in the air. And forget about keepin' your eyes open, less you wanna get an eyeball full of sand.

They got one of those anemometer thingamajiggers over at the Kitty Hawk Life Saving Station that spins round and measures the speed of the wind. Well, it got up to 90 mile per hour, and then the wind done up and BLEW THE ANEMOMETER AWAY!

That's ONE way to measure wind speed. If your anemometer blows away, you can bet you got some hard wind. Don't need no anemometer anyhow. Just go outside and try to hold a hat on your head.

Then come the rains. I thought all of Albemarle Sound up and fell on our heads. When it was done, I went over to Kitty Hawk to see the damage. There was pieces of boats and junk all over the beach. No sign of them Wright brothers. It'd be a shame if them nice fellers got shipwrecked and drownded.

July 11, 1901

Thursday evening. I got the word from my old chum Elijah that Mr. Wilbur and Mr. Orville showed up at Captain Tate's house, wet as a couple of dunked cats. I couldn't venture over there cause I had to help mama bail water out of the kitchen.

Elijah says he hears tell the Wrights are gonna stay in North Carolina longer this year. And he says this time they're gonna build a permanent camp with a wood shed. But of course, everybody knows Elijah is a born liar, so it might all be fibs.

I'll say this much for those Wrights. If Mr. Wilbur and Mr. Orville are willin' to come back to these parts after last year, they ain't no quitters. That's for durn sure.

July 12, 1901

Friday morning. It was still rainin' a trifle, but I rode my bicycle to Captain Tate's house in Kitty Hawk anyhow to say howdy. Mr. Wilbur and Mr. Orville seemed glad to see me. Mr. Orville says he would of thought I would of got me a pair of shoes by now, and I told him what's the point of wearin' shoes, because then you gotta put 'em on and take 'em off all the time? When you go barefoot, you don't need that botheration.

While we was jawin', down from the upstairs comes Captain Tate's wife, Miz Addie, and her little gals, Irene and Pauline. They can't be no mor'n 3 or 4 years old. They was both wearin' these fancy matchin' white dresses like they was all dressed up for church.

"Do you like our new dresses?" Pauline says, spinnin' round to show off for Mr. Wilbur and Mr. Orville.

The Wrights say, "They're very pretty," or some such thing.

"Mommy sewed them," Irene brags.

"Yes, I made them from the wing covering of the glider you left in the sand last year," said Miz Addie.

I couldn't hardly believe that Miz Addie woulda tore the cloth right off the wings and made it into dresses for her little gals. I thought Mr. Wilbur was gonna be sore, but he just bowed all polite like and says, "Well, it looks better on the girls than it did on our glider."

It was still rainin', but Mr. Wilbur and Mr. Orville was anxious to set up their camp. First they picked a site a few hunnerd foot north of Big Kill Devil Hill. That way, they wouldn't have to carry their flyin' machine so far when they were a-fixin' to fly it. Captain Tate and his horse Don Keyhoaty helped tote the lumber and gear out to the site.

It was no fun settin' up the tent in the rain, but we did it. Then we sat in the tent and watched the clouds. Everybody was thirsty, but nobody wanted to venture all the way back to Captain Tate's house for water. Mr. Orville got the bright idea of catchin' the rainwater with the tent roof and fillin' a bottle with it. It tasted a little soapy cause they had rubbed soap on the tent so it wouldn't get mildew, but it was tolerable. When the rain commenced to stop, they drove a pump pipe into the ground outside the tent till they hit water.

July 13, 1901

Still rainin'. The tent is big enough for four or five people to live in, but it ain't big enough for the new flyin' machine they're gonna build. So Mr. Wilbur and Mr. Orville are fixin' to build themselves a wood shed.

When they showed me the plans they drew up, I said whoa! This is SOME SHED. 25 foot long and 16 foot wide. Tall enough for a grown man to stand in. This year, they ain't here for no vacation. These Wright Brothers are fixin' to stick round awhile.

Captain Tate had to go to work at the lifesaving station. Mr. Wilbur framed up the building with lumber, and I set to work sawin' and nailin' and so on with Mr. Orville. He was all mommicked that I was gonna step on a nail or something and get hurt. He kept sayin' do you ALWAYS walk around barefoot and I says well, sure, and showed him the sand spurs on the bottom of my feet. He says I should wear shoes anyhow.

There was this nail stickin' up from a board, and Mr. Orville went to hammer it down, but I went over first and just pushed the nail down with my heel.

"How did you do that?" Mr. Orville asked, like I done magic or something.

"It's simple," I say. "I don't wash my feet. Toughens 'em up so they ain't timid like most folks feet." He thought that was curious. It put his mind at ease, and he didn't trouble me about gettin' hurt no more.

While we was workin' on the shed, Mr. Wilbur and Mr. Orville kept talkin' over and over about the "flyin' problem." Finally I says what's the flyin' problem and Mr. Wilbur says the flying problem boils down to the fact that we humans have problems flying.

We took a rest from work, and they set down on the beach to try and learn me the flyin' problem. Mr. Wilbur, he says an aeroplane ain't that much different from a bicycle. Both of 'em has what he calls three axes of motion. But they ain't like axes you use to cut down a tree. They're like rules of movement or something.

The first axis of motion is called pitch, which ain't like a baseball pitch. Pitch is when the front of the flyin' machine goes up and down. Like when you ride a bicycle up and down a hill.

The second axis of motion is called roll, which ain't like when you roll a ball. Roll is when the one wing tilts up and the other one tilts down. Like when you lean a bicycle into a turn.

The third axis of motion is called yaw, which ain't like what you do when you're sleepy. Yaw is when the front of the flyin' machine moves left and right. Like when you turn the handlebars of a bicycle.

Those are the three ways a flyin' machine can turn. It's easy on a bicycle. But if you wanna fly, Mr. Wilbur tells me, you gotta control all 3 of 'em or you crack up. And if you crack up, you got a REAL flyin' problem.

Makes sense, I spose. But I still don't know how they're gonna SOLVE the flyin' problem. And I ain't sure they do neither.

July 14, 1901

Sunday. I didn't even bother goin' over to Kill Devil Hill cause I know Mr. Wilbur and Mr. Orville's daddy won't let 'em work on Sunday. Besides, it's rainin' again.

Chloe Beasley sees me and says do I want to come over to her house and play with her dolls. I say no, I do NOT want to play with your durn dolls cause dolls is for girls. She started in cryin'. So I went over and played with her dolls a whit to make her happy again.

July 15, 1901

Monday. I done some thinkin' about the flyin' problem while I was layin' in bed last night. That pitch, roll, and yaw business makes some sense, leastways as far as controllin' the flyin' machine goes. But I was still iffy about one thing: What's gonna get the machine up in the air in the first place? Ain't no use learnin' how to control the thing if you can't get it up in the air.

Birds got flappin' wings to get 'em in the air. Mr. Wilbur and Mr. Orville already told me humans ain't strong enough to flap wings and fly. So what are they fixin' to do?

When I rode over to Kill Devil, Mr. Wilbur was hammerin' away at the shed, but Mr. Orville was sittin' down and lookin' right peekish. I say, what's wrong and he says he's bad off on account of that soapy rainwater he drunk the other day. His stomach is all quamished.

Even though he was unwell, Mr. Orville was a-willin' to learn me about the flyin' problem. So I say to him, what's gonna get the durn flyin' machine up in the air?

Mr. Orville takes up a screwdriver and he starts drawin' a

picture in the sand. It looks like he's a-drawin' a banana shot by arrows, but he says it's the wing of an aeroplane with wind rushin' by it.

He says that when wind shoots past the wing, because it's curved down a whit, there's less air pressure on the top of the wing than there is on the underside. That causes lift, and the wing goes up whether you want it to or not.

Well, he might as well be talkin' Greek. I didn't know what air pressure was anyways, and I told him so. Mr. Orville picked up a piece of paper and held it up to his mouth like he was gonna take a bite out of it. He says

he's gonna blow air across the top of the paper and asks do I think the paper will go up or down. I say down of course, which makes sense.

So he blows over the top, and the paper heists UP! That's something, innit? You coulda knocked me down with a goose feather! He says it's the same thing that will make the wing of a flyin' machine go up.

Well, I never DID quite get the smart of it, but I reckon he and his brother maybe ain't so crazy after all.

Even though Mr. Orville was feelin' poorly, he got up to help Mr. Wilbur on the shed. So did I. By the end of the day, it was finished. There was two big doors on each side that could swing open wide enough for the flyin' machine to get in and out. There was enough room for a little workshop, too. It was a fine building, nearbout as nice as some folks houses in these parts.

Mr. Wilbur and Mr. Orville were glad the shed was done, cause now they can start buildin' their new flyin' machine. Not only that, but they says they got some visitors comin' shortly to watch their experiments. I say who, and they say they never met these visitors afore, but one is a doctor and the other two are scientists interested in flyin'.

They sound like spies to me and I say so. I say bringin' in more dingbatters is a bad idea cause they're gonna steal your secrets and go off and build their own flying machines. Mr. Wilbur says he ain't got no secrets worth stealin', leastways not yet. I still say bringin' in more dingbatters is a bad idea.

July 16, 1901

More rain. They started buildin' the new flyin' machine today anyway.

First thing I notice is there's no engine. So I say where's the engine and they say there ain't no engine, it's a glider. And I say, another glider? What do you need another durn glider for? You DONE that already. Why don't you build your aeroplane, stick an engine on her, and see if she'll fly?

Mr. Wilbur, he says nope, they got to learn how to fly the thing afore they can build it. Well, it seemed all backwards to me.

Mr. Orville says flyin' an aeroplane ain't like drivin' an automobile. If you mess up while you're flyin', you can't just hit the brake and start again. True enough, I s'pose.

They commenced to buildin' the glider. One thing I'd been noticin' was that these fellers was pretty handy. I thought city boys didn't even know how to hammer a nail, but Mr. Wilbur and Mr. Orville work with wood and metal like they was born with tools in their hands. I guess that's why they run a bicycle shop.

I say your Daddy learned you well and they say their daddy had nothin' to do with it. He is a man of the cloth, and I don't mean he shoots billiards. They say it was their MAMA who learned 'em how to build and fix things, may she rest in peace. She died when Mr. Orville was 18.

One winter she built 'em a sled, which is pretty impressive. Don't know of no woman round here, and hardly any men, who can build a sled. Course, we ain't got much snow round here, so who needs a sled anyway?

They both looked sad talkin' about their mama, so I didn't ask nothin' more about her.

Last year when the Wrights come, it was dead sure that Mr. Wilbur was the boss and Mr. Orville was his helper. This year things are diffr'nt. Mr. Orville is just as likely to be tellin' Mr.

Wilbur what to do as it is for Mr. Wilbur to be tellin' Mr. Orville what do to. They work together, with no boss.

By suppertime, they knocked off work and took a walk up the beach to watch the gulls fly. They would stare up in the sky and jaw about the flyin' problem some more, like they ain't been talkin' about it all day already.

Then, with no warnin', Mr. Orville would run down to the water edge, flappin' his arms up and down, jumpin', and makin' bird noises. He looked like he was havin' some fine fun. I tell you, one minute I reckon these Wright brothers got it all figured out, and the next minute I reckon they're loons.

July 18, 1901

Thursday. I get to the Wright camp, and this feller I never seen afore is there jawin' with Mr. Wilbur and Mr. Orville. They tell me his name is Edward Huffaker and he's from Tennessee. This Huffaker feller has been workin' with gliders for years and even went to college to study physics, whatever that is.

Well, he didn't look like no college boy to me. Huffaker was ugly as a mud fence, and he had a cigar in his mouth that he only took out when he had to spit, which was frequent. Then he puts it back. When Huffaker said his first cuss word, I caught Mr. Orville lookin' at Mr. Wilbur like he smelled a skunk.

"You reckon he's a spy?" I asked, when Huffaker went off to the woods to do his business. Mr. Wilbur and Mr. Orville didn't believe so. But I reckon they didn't like Huffaker much neither.

Huffaker brought along a bunch of long, fat paper tubes with him. When he told me he was fixin' to make 'em into a flyin' machine of his OWN, I almost bust out laughin'. I'd make easy money bettin' THAT thing won't fly a foot. He says he spent A THOUSAND DOLLARS on it so far!

There's no room in the shed for two planes, so I don't know what Huffaker's gonna do with his paper tubes after he puts 'em together. Lucky for him, it stopped a-rainin' at last.

July 19, 1901

As soon as it stopped a-rainin', it got hot and the skeeters come. It was almost like Huffaker brought 'em with him from Tennessee.

Now, I seen skeeters afore. You can't live on the Banks and not be used to skeeters in late summer and early fall. They're somewhat bothersome, but usually tolerable.

This was diffr'nt. When I got near Kill Devil Hill, the air sounded like a buzz saw. Skeeters was everywhere, coverin' the sand and the tent like a black cloud. You could swat 'em and kill 'em, but a heap more would just come and take their place. There was so many of 'em that they darkened the sun. I never seen nothing like it.

I called to Mr. Wilbur and Mr. Orville and heard 'em in the tent. I go inside and there they were in their beds wrapped in blankets with towels wrapped round their heads coverin' up everything but their noses. It was hot and they was sweatin' like pigs. They had bites all over. Huffaker was in the other bed, mad as a wet settin' hen and cussin' a blue streak. Didn't look like they was gonna do no work on the glider today.

"Johnny, go get us some mosquito netting!" Mr. Wilbur shouted.

"Skeeter nettin' ain't gonna work," I told him, but he says get it anyway.

I rode to the Kitty Hawk Life Saving Station and Mr. Tate give me all the netting I could tote. I bring it back to the Wright camp and wrap it round the bunks. It helped somewhat. They was able to take off the blankets, anyway.

"They chewed us right through our underwear and socks," Mr. Orville says, swattin' the dead skeeters off his bed.

For a minute, I thought the netting done the trick. But then the skeeters, like always, found an opening and got inside. Soon Mr. Wilbur and Mr. Orville were swattin' and sweatin' and scratchin' and Huffaker was spittin' and cussin'.

"Skeeters are small enough to fit thru skeeter netting," I told 'em. "But then they take a bite of you and it fattens 'em up. They get too big to get back out of the holes in the net. That's the problem."

"Shut up!" shouted Huffaker, along with some other things I can't write down or mama would whip me.

Mr. Wilbur and Mr. Orville said this was the last time they are gonna come to the Outer Banks in the middle of the summer. I was afraid they might pack up right then and venture back to Ohio. Huffaker said it was the last time he was gonna come down here period.

The Banks is not always the best place in the world to live. I reckon that is why not many people live here. Leastways those of us who do live here got plenty of room, I'll say that much. You take the bad with the good.

There was nothin I could do to help, so I went home. The skeeters ain't so thick in Nags Head.

July 20, 1901

I rode to the Wright camp round noon, and at first I think the shed is on fire. Turns out they drug over some old tree trunks and set 'em ablaze to drive the skeeters away. It worked, somewhat.

Only problem was the fire made the heat even hotter and the smoke so thick a person couldn't hardly breathe. But I reckon they decided smoke and heat were more tolerable than skeeters. Leastways now they could work on buildin' their glider.

After a while, you couldn't do nothing but laugh at all them skeeters anyway. "Now I know what happened to the lost colony of Roanoke," Mr. Orville says as he's sawin' wood. "The mosquitos ate them!" Huffaker cursed. Mr. Wilbur didn't say nothing. Nobody laughed but me.

Huffaker has proven to be a nasty feller. When we stop for lunch, he says he ain't gonna do the cookin' or cleanin' up after cause he ain't the hired help. I wished Mr. Wilbur or Mr. Orville would of frapped him, but they just did the cookin' and cleanin' THEMSELVES. They ain't the fightin' kind.

When they work on their new glider, Huffaker goes off to work on his paper tube plane. It's got five wings, with parts goin' off everywhichway. What a joke that thing is!

When Huffaker ain't in earshot, Mr. Wilbur calls the paper tube plane "THE THOUSAND-DOLLAR BEAUTY." And he don't mean that in a nice way.

July 23, 1901

The glider is nearbout finished.

July 25, 1901

George Spratt must be a good luck charm, cause as soon as HE showed up, the skeeters went away.

When the skeeters go, WHERE do they go, anyhow? That's what I was wonderin'. Who cares, as long as they go somewheres ELSE. And they went, just as sudden as they come. Everybody cheered up considerable.

Mr. Spratt, I mean Doc Spratt, is a doctor mostly. But he's interested in flyin', too, so he asked Mr. Wilbur and Mr. Orville if he could come down here from his home in Pennsylvania and lend a hand. I reckon they figured it wouldn't be a bad idea to have a doctor handy in case of an emergency.

"You sure this Doc Spratt feller ain't a spy?" I asked Mr. Wilbur, and he says sure he's sure. But I reckon Mr. Wilbur wouldn't know a spy from a bucket of beets anyhow. If somebody is good at spyin', you can't tell. It's not like they walk round wearin' a sign round their neck that says SPY on it.

Doc Spratt is a tall, thin man, and much sunnier than Huffaker, that's for sure. First thing he says to me is you want to hear a joke and I say yes, and he says what about and I say flyin' machines and he says he don't know no flyin' machine jokes, but how about this one

WHAT ANIMAL FALLS FROM THE CLOUDS?

I say I don't know.

A REINDEER.

I say I don't get it and he says REINDEER . . . REINDEER. He said reindeer a few times afore I figured out what was so funny. Even then it weren't all THAT funny. But Doc Spratt threw back his head and laughed like it was the funniest joke ever.

Mr. Wilbur and Mr. Orville took a likin' to Doc Spratt right away, unlike Huffaker, who continues to be bothersome. This mornin' he called the Wrights fools cause they wear church clothes for hard work. I could tell Mr. Wilbur didn't like that, though he didn't say nothin'. Huffaker wears the same shirt every day, and it is startin' to smell powerful goaty.

We worked all afternoon on the glider, which is takin' shape. Huffaker says it will never get off the ground. Doc Spratt keeps sayin', It WILL work! It MUST work! It can't HELP but work!

After dinner I spied Doc Spratt a-layin' on the beach and lookin' up in the sky. He's got a fishin' pole stuck in the sand but the line ain't even in the water. So I venture over and say what are you fishin' for and he says he ain't fishin' for nothin', he's watchin' the birds fly.

So I say what do you got a fishin' pole for and he says folks think you're crazy if they catch you just layin' on the ground watchin' birds. But if you got a fishin' pole next to you, they reckon you're doin' something worthwhile. Makes sense to me.

Doc Spratt told me a couple of jokes, but I can't write 'em here cause they are dirty. I didn't get the jokes, but I laughed anyhow so Doc wouldn't think me a little boy.

July 26, 1901

They finished buildin' the new glider. This one's nearbout twice as big as the last one, 22 foot across the wings and 98 pound. Mr. Orville says it HAD to be bigger so it would have more liftin' power.

Don't make no sense to me. Seems the bigger and more heavy you build it, the HARDER it's gonna be to get off the

ground. But Mr. Wilbur and Mr. Orville seem to know what they are doin'.

They put a new control system on this glider. They got rid of the foot control and put on what Mr. Wilbur calls a HIP CRADLE. When you're a-layin' on it, you move your hips to the right to warp the right wing down, and you move left to warp the left wing down. That is, after you get the thing up in the air, which ain't likely.

They say they're gonna take it out tomorrow for some tests. I ask if I can get a ride and they say no cause it ain't perfected yet. Shucks, it looks perfected enough to me, but nothin' doin'.

July 27, 1901

Saturday. No skeeters at all. Captain Tate and some of the

surfmen from the Kitty Hawk Life Saving Station come over to the Wright camp. Looked to me like they rushed through their work so they could fool round with the flyin' machine.

Mr. Wilbur takes out his anemometer and says the wind is blowin' only 13 mile per hour and they need 17 mile per hour to take off. He worked it all out with a pencil in his little notebook.

So all the men carried the glider up to the top of Big Hill so as to let gravity help get some more speed.

Mr. Wilbur climbed on the glider, like always. Mr. Orville and Captain Tate picked it up by the wingtips. Some of the other men grabbed the back. Mr. Wilbur had 'em turn the thing round till it was facin' the wind. Huffaker was put in charge of the anemometer and some other thingamadodgers.

"Allright, go!" Mr. Wilbur shouted.

The men let out a whoop and run the thing down the dune. It heisted up a few foot for maybe a second, but then it dives for the sand like a shot buzzard and skids to a stop. We all run down to the bottom of the hill to see if Mr. Wilbur is hurt.

"I need to move the center of gravity backwards," is all Mr. Wilbur has to say. He looks none the worse for wear 'cept for the sand on his face, and the glider looks like nothin' is broken.

We try again and the same thing happens. And again too, and six more times after that. Each time, Mr. Wilbur moved back a trifle, till he could barely reach the controls. Didn't make much difference. The glider didn't want to go up nohow.

After eight tries the men were so tuckered from totin' the glider up the dune I was afraid they might just up and leave. But Mr. Orville invited 'em to lunch, and I caught a mess of fish for him to cook up. We had a contest to see who could spit the bones furthest. Huffaker won. Doc Spratt said Huffaker is so good at spittin' cause he practices all day, even when there ain't no contest.

We go up the hill again after lunch and Mr. Wilbur is sore cause Huffaker left the anemometer and the other thingamajiggers just layin' there in the sand the whole time we was eatin'. Huffaker didn't apologize or nothin'. He just acted like it weren't no big deal. Mr. Wilbur looked like he was gonna blow his top, but he didn't.

They did some more glides after lunch, and a few of 'em reached the bottom of the hill and more. But Mr. Wilbur couldn't hold her level. He was workin' the elevator, but the glider was buckin' up and down like a wild horse the whole way down the hill.

On one glide we all thought Mr. Wilbur was a goner. He took off same as usual, but when the glider turned up, it just kept turnin' up till it was headin' straight up in the air. It stopped nearbout 20 foot up and just hung there for a whit. Then it fell backwards.

"Jump out, Will!" Mr. Orville screamed.

It was too late for that. The glider dropped straight down and hit the sand like a critter full of buckshot. Mr. Wilbur was still shook up when we got to him, but he weren't dead nor even hurt bad. Mr. Orville was proud that the glider come through the crash with nary a scratch too.

Mr. Wilbur and Mr. Orville could of gone on, but the surf-men had to leave, so they called it a day. It was 17 glides, all told.

Mr. Orville said the best glide went 315 foot and stayed up 19 second. That beats anything anybody else ever done, but it weren't good enough.

"We're not here to set records," Mr. Wilbur says. "We're

here to build a practical flying machine."

I pondered askin' for a ride at the end of the day, but Mr. Wilbur didn't look like he was in no mood for it. So I took off for Nags Head and made it home just in time for supper.

> During all the flights we had made up to this time we had kept close to the ground, in order that, in case we met any new and mysterious phenomenon, we could make a safe landing. With only one life to spend we did not consider it advisable to attempt to explore mysteries at such great height from the ground that a fall would put an end to our investigations and leave the mystery unsolved.

—Wilbur Wright

July 28, 1901

That little squirt Chloe Beasley saw me, and she says how come you go over to Kitty Hawk most every day? Is the fishin' that good over there?

I says I ain't a-goin' to Kitty Hawk, I'm a-goin' to Kill Devil Hill.

Same difference, she says. What are you doin' there, meetin' some girl?

I says no, I ain't meetin' no girl.

It's none of Chloe's business, but I tell her anyway that I go to help Mr. Wilbur and Mr. Orville with their flyin' machine. She stares at me, eyes wide open, and says, Johnny Moore, are you possessed by the devil? I say no, and she says everybody knows them dingbatters from Ohio is touched in the head.

I tell her truthful that I ain't so sure no more. Maybe they're touched in the head and maybe they ain't. Maybe they really ARE gonna fly.

Chloe Beasley throws her head back and laughs like I told a joke. THEY FIX BICYCLES! she says, like that explains everything. She says I oughtn't be a-wastin' my time round 'em when there are fish to be caught right here in Nags Head.

I reckon I'm old enough to do what I wanna do and fish where I wanna fish without some little girl tellin' me. I come and go as I please.

July 30, 1901

That crack-up the other day sure mommicked Mr. Wilbur horribly, cause now he don't want to get in the glider nohow. When I rode to the Wright camp, he and Mr. Orville were flyin' the thing as a kite.

Then they took the machine apart, tryin' to figure out what was wrong. They tore out the elevator and made it smaller, but that didn't help much. Next they fussed with the wings. That didn't help much neither.

"I'm afraid that our calculations may be wrong," Mr. Wilbur said.

After each glide Mr. Wilbur and Mr. Orville would write a bunch of numbers down in their notebook and talk things over. They keep tryin' new things, but nothin' helps. This new glider works worse than the one from last year. Sometimes Mr. Wilbur just goes and sits down on the sand by hisself till Mr. Orville comes over and tries to pep him up or Doc Spratt tells him a joke.

Huffaker ain't helpin' matters. It's plain as the nose on your face he thinks both of the Wrights are dummies. When they ain't round, he badmouths 'em and calls 'em THOSE BICYCLE MECHANICS. Today he sat down on their big camera like it was a chair. Mr. Wilbur looked like he was just about to faint, but he didn't say nothin'. He just waited till Huffaker got up, and put the camera in the shed. Mr. Wilbur sure knows how to hold his temper better than any man I ever met, that's for sure. If Huffaker had sat on MY camera, I'd a frapped him one.

August 2, 1901

We was out on the dunes with the glider when I get the feelin' somebody is watchin'. I turn round and sure enough there's 3 or 4 heads poppin' out from behind the trees distant. Soon as I point and tell Mr. Wilbur and Mr. Orville to look, the heads duck down. A minute later I look again and there they are. Heads with binoculars.

"I reckon somebody's a-spyin' on you," I say.

Doc Spratt says they're most likely some local girls on the lookout for husbands, but I reckon that was just one of his jokes. I say I can run off into the woods and scare 'em away, if you like. Huffaker offers to SHOOT 'em. But Mr. Wilbur and Mr. Orville say they're prob'ly reporters and leave 'em be, cause there's nothin' worth reportin' anyhow.

If report is to be credited, there is building on an unfrequented part of Carolina's coast an airship . . . . An Ohio inventor with two companions and fellow-Workmen . . . have been there busied for some time in the perfection of a machine with which they expect to solve the problem of aerial navigation. The utmost secrecy is being maintained in regard to the same and the aerial craft itself is kept within an enclosed structure. Scant courtesy is shown and but meager information doled out to the few inhabitants who have been led by curiosity to this isolated spot.

Elizabeth City North Carolinian, **August 1, 1901**

August 5, 1901

Went a-fishin' in the mornin'. Caught a mess of fatback. When I get to the Wright camp round noon, there's another feller there besides Huffaker and Doc Spratt. He's an old man, maybe 70 years out, I suspect. He's a baldy like Mr. Wilbur 'cept for patches of white hair on the sides. He got a white goatee and mustache, and he's wearin' a cape. I don't know who the feller is, but I reckon he ain't gonna be much help totin' the glider up the dunes. He was walkin' slow as molasses runnin' uphill on a cold day.

The old feller was talkin' English, but in a French soundin' voice. Mr. Wilbur, Mr. Orville, Doc Spratt, and Huffaker was sittin' at his feet just listenin' like they was a bunch of schoolboys. I figured this feller must be important, so I pull out my book and write down his exact words.

"For centuries man has dreamed of flight. It demonstrates our natural desire for the ultimate freedom, to break free of the bounds of gravity. To be bound to the earth is to be held captive, like an animal in a cage."

Nobody said nothin'. I was writin' as fast as I could to keep up.

"If man can build a practical flying machine, it will be perhaps the most dramatic achieve-

ment in the human experience, just as important as the discovery of fire, gravity, or the invention of the wheel! And if man can fly, what can he NOT do? The possibilities are unlimited! Think of it, we will be able to move in three dimensions. Can you imagine how that will change our world? Who knows what wonders we will be able to create in this new century? The sky, my friends, is the limit!"

Well, it sounded like a lot of gas to me. The old feller sure did like to hear the sound of his own voice. He didn't shut his yap till Mr. Orville give him some grub.

Mr. Wilbur says howdy to me and tells me the old feller's

name is Octave Chanute. Shucks, I never met nobody named OCTAVE afore, I can tell you that.

"He don't look like no flyer to me," I says. "You think he's one of them spies I saw in the woods?"

Mr. Wilbur says I think EVERYBODY is a spy, and I say, I do not, just suspicious lookin' fellers like this old coot Chanute. While he and Doc Spratt and Huffaker eat, I keep thinkin' Mr. Wilbur and Mr. Orville would get a heap more done if all these dingbatters would get out of here. 'Tween feedin' 'em and makin' chitchat, it uses up the whole day.

"Why don't you tell this Chanute feller to get out of here?" I say to Mr. Orville while the others was cleanin' up.

"Octave Chanute is the leading aeronautical expert in the world," he says. "We invited him here to observe our experiments."

"Expert, eh?" says I. "Well, what did HE ever fly?"

"He is a very famous civil engineer," Mr. Orville says. "He built the first bridge across the Missouri River."

That's all well and good, but I ain't never seen no flyin' bridge, and I reckon I never will.

August 8, 1901

Chloe Beasley turned 6 today, but I was lucky cause her mama took her to visit her grandma, so I didn't have to go to no little girl birthday party like I did last year.

August 9, 1901

Mr. Wilbur and Mr. Orville bootlick this old coot Chanute like he is king of the sand dunes or something. Chanute wants to see some glides, so they tote the glider out and start a-showin' it off for him. They got one glide nearbout 400 foot, and Chanute acts like they landed on the durn moon.

Chanute is particular interested in the wing warpin' system, so he tells Mr. Wilbur and Mr. Orville to try a few turns. Well, they ain't barely tried turnin' yet, but they don't want to disappoint the old coot. So we tote the glider up the hill. Mr. Wilbur clum on, and we let her fly.

Now, the way I know it, the glider is s'posed to tilt on a turn like you tilt on a bicycle. Well, Mr. Wilbur warped the wings and tried to tilt it, but nothin' doin'. The thing sorta skidded in the air, the back slippin' sideways. Halfway down the hill the left wingtip dipped down and nicked the sand. The glider dug in and spun round like a pinwheel. Next thing we know, Mr. Wilbur goes flyin' clear out of the thing.

We all run down the hill, even old Chanute huffin' and puffin' like he was about to keel over. Mr. Wilbur was layin' in the sand 10 foot from the glider. He was okay, 'cept his leg was skinned and he has some bruises and cuts on his face and nose. The glider needed some doctorin' too.

Instead of cussin' like anyone else would, all's Mr. Wilbur says as we help him up is, "I think perhaps we're not ready to make turns."

The brothers was disencouraged that they let down the great man, but Chanute is all excited, sayin' they was doin' great at attackin' the flyin' problem.

"The greatest minds the world has produced tried to solve this problem and failed miserably," he says as we tote the glider back to the shed for repairs. "Thomas Edison hasn't been able to solve it. Alexander Graham Bell hasn't been able to solve it. Even the great Professor Langley has yet to be successful."

Edison and Bell I heard of. But I never heard of no Langley.

"Who's Professor Langley?" I say.

"My dear boy," Chanute says, "Professor Samuel Pierpont Langley is the head of the Smithsonian Institution in Washington. He is perhaps the most famous scientist in the world."

"Well, he ain't famous to me."

"Professor Langley has already demonstrated a steam-powered model aerodrome that has flown a half a mile," Chanute says. "He is working very hard to build a full size model with a human pilot."

Here I was thinkin' Mr. Wilbur and Mr. Orville was a couple of crackpots with the crazy idea of buildin' a flyin' machine. Turns out lots of folks are tryin' to do the same durn thing.

"Young man," Chanute tells me, "this is very much a race for the sky. SOMEONE will figure out the secret of flight. It is merely a matter of time. I believe that. The inventor of the first practical flying machine will go down in history and be remembered forever. That is why inventors all over the world are working on the flying problem at this very moment. From my observations the Wright brothers and Professor Langley are in the lead."

It subsequently became known that Professor Langley was still secretly at work on a machine for the United States Government.

—Orville and Wilbur Wright

August 11, 1901

That old coot Chanute and Doc Spratt had to go home, so we walked 'em over to Kitty Hawk to catch a boat to the mainland. Chanute I could do without, but I was sorry to see Doc Spratt go. He told me one more joke before saying good-bye. Something about throwing a clock out the window to see time fly. I didn't get it, but I laughed anyway.

Mr. Wilbur and Mr. Orville were apologizin' up and down for draggin' Chanute all the way to North Carolina and not makin' much progress.

"How much progress has ANYONE made in the 400 years since Leonardo da Vinci imagined a flying machine?" Chanute tells 'em. "You gentlemen are close to the solution. Perhaps closer than you know."

"We would appreciate it if you would refrain from telling others the details of our experiments," Mr. Wilbur says to Chanute.

"Your secrets are safe with me."

"That's not it," Mr. Wilbur says. "We would rather the world not know of our failure."

"It is always best to keep one's interest in human flight to one's self," Chanute says as he gets on the boat. "Unless we want people to think of us as lunatics. Do not despair, gentlemen. It will take teams of scientists and engineers working together to solve the flying problem. No one man can do it."

After the boat pulled away, Mr. Orville says, "But TWO men might."

After they left, I went back to Kill Devil Hill to help Mr. Wilbur and Mr. Orville fix their busted glider.

August 15, 1901

It rained last night. When I got to the Wright camp, Huffaker was runnin' round like a crazy man tryin' to cover up his paper tube glider. It weren't no use. The thing crumpled like a house of straw. Huffaker was angry as a bull. He just loaded up his stuff and went to Kitty Hawk. Didn't even say good-bye. He has left, and I hope he stays gone.

After Huffaker left, Mr. Orville says one of his blankets is missin' from his bed. He says Huffaker must of took it by mistake, but I don't think it was no mistake. That feller was just hard down mean.

"Was he a spy?" I ask.

"I don't think so," Mr. Wilbur says. "Just a very disagreeable man. We won't invite him back here."

They seemed happier now that all them guests was gone. The glider was fixed, so we loaded it up with sandbags and flew it as a kite.

Then they tried some glides, but the thing wouldn't go more than 200 foot afore crackin' up. Even I didn't want to ride on the thing, for fear of killin' myself.

Mr. Wilbur and Mr. Orville said they had a heap of problems to solve and they didn't even know where to start cause they didn't know what was wrong. Mr. Wilbur is the melancholy type, and he looked down as ever.

We was ready to haul the glider back to the shed for the night when this odd-lookin' feller with a beard comes a-walkin' up the beach. He's totin' a big box in both arms.

"Are you the gentlemen who are building a flying machine?" he asks. "I read about you in the newspaper."

Mr. Wilbur and Mr. Orville say yes.

"I have something you may be interested in," the bearded

feller says, and opens the box. There are a bunch of wheels and wires and stuff inside.

"What is it?" Mr. Wilbur says.

"It's the first practical perpetual motion machine," the feller says, and I see both Wrights roll their eyes at each other. "It will run forever at 100% efficiency with no source of fuel. I thought that perhaps you gentlemen might want to team up in business and become my partners."

"No, thank you," Mr. Wilbur says.

Then, after the feller is down the beach a bit, Mr. Wilbur says, "He probably has as much chance of success as we do."

August 22, 1901

It rained for four days, so I knew there'd be no flyin' at Kill Devil Hill. When I finally get back there, Mr. Wilbur and Mr. Orville are packin' up their camp.

"You leavin' so soon?" I ask. "I thought you was gonna stay at least into September."

"We are finished," Mr. Wilbur says. "Two years wasted. Why should we succeed when so many other experimenters, with better education and funding, have failed? Either our calculations are wrong, or there IS no solution to the flying problem. Perhaps man simply isn't destined to fly."

"At least we weren't killed," Mr. Orville says, tryin' to smile.

"I doubt that man will fly in my lifetime," Mr. Wilbur says. "Not within a thousand years will man ever fly."

Captain Tate come with Don Quixote (I just found out Keyhoaty is spelled Quixote. Don't that beat all?) to help cart their things to the wharf. When we said good-bye, I didn't think

I would ever see the Wright brothers back in Kitty Hawk again.

September 7, 1901

Little Chloe Beasley comes a-runnin' up to me hootin' and hollerin' like a house on fire. I say, what's wrong and she says SOMEBODY TRIED TO KILL PRESIDENT MCKINLEY!

At first I think she's joshin', but then she is cryin', so I know she ain't lyin'. She says the President was shot in Buffalo, New York. Chloe says it looks like he's a-gonna die. She thinks she knows everything. She ain't never even shot a gun in her life, so what does she know about it?

September 15, 1901

They are burying President McKinley today. Vice President Roosevelt is the new President of the United States. Chloe Beasley says he's the youngest president ever. That little squirt thinks she knows everything.

October 6, 1901

Well, the Orphans had a rotten season, like ALWAYS. They only won 53 games and lost 86. It says in the newspapers they're so bad they're a-changin' their name. Next year they're gonna be called The Chicago Cubs. What a dumb name for a team.

Book 3: 1902
THE SECRET OF FLIGHT

Flight by machines heavier than air is unpractical and insignificant if not utterly impossible.

—Simon Newcomb,
astronomer at the U.S. Naval Observatory, 1902

January 1, 1902

I walked up along the beach to Kill Devil Hill today to see what the Wright camp looked like. There was a terrible storm last week with lightnin' that turned night into day and burned down just about every telegraph pole tween Nags Head and Kitty Hawk.

The camp was nearbout wrecked. The wind blew the foundation right out from under the shed. The walls are still standin', but just barely. The wood floor is buried under a foot of sand. Stuff was all over. There was a few scrawny lookin' chickens runnin' round, searchin' for something to eat. It was sad to look at.

Maybe that's the end of it. After the way Mr. Wilbur and Mr. Orville left in August, I don't reckon we'll be seein 'em round here no more. They looked like they gave up on solvin' that flyin' problem they was always jawing about.

Who knows? Maybe that Langley feller beat 'em with HIS aeroplane. Didn't read nothin' in the papers about no flyin' machine, though.

Only good thing is if the Wrights don't show up this year, nobody will be pokin' fun at me for goin' round and helpin' 'em.

March 6, 1902

Happy birthday to ME. Mama says she don't care whether I write in the book or not no more cause I'm 17 now and 17-year-olds don't need to go to school anyways. But I reckon I'll write in the book if something worth writin' about happens.

Mama says if I'm gonna write in the durn book, I might as well write right, with the right spelling and grammar and all. She has started in givin' me grammar lessons herself, like when to

say DON'T and when to say DOESN'T and when to say
NOBODY and when to say ANYBODY. Mama says it won't be
long afore I set out on my own in the world and she don't want
me soundin' like some dumb cracker. I mean DOESN'T.

I say, "I don't sound like no dumb cracker," and she says,
"Yes, you do too, cause you just said NO DUMB CRACKER
'stead of A DUMB CRACKER."

I don't like these grammar lessons one bit.

April 19, 1902

The Cubs—how am I gonna get used to callin 'em Cubs?—
are lookin' good so far. They whipped them Cincinnati Reds 9-5
yesterday. They got this new shortstop named Joe Tinker who
they say got hands soft as pillows. Maybe with Tinker and
Chance together they got a chance.

August 29, 1902

Mama sent me to Kitty Hawk to buy some sewin' thread,
and who do I see at the wharf but Mr. Wilbur and Mr. Orville!
They was powerful happy to see me, and likewise from my side.
I growed six inches since last year and am nearbout as tall as Mr.
Orville now, and he says soon I will be as big as Mr. Wilbur. They
was totin' lots of stuff. Not just flyin' machine stuff, but also an
oven, a bicycle, and a barrel of gasoline.

"Our calculations were wrong," Mr. Orville says as I walk
'em out to their camp, or what was left of it, anyway. "That's why
we couldn't get enough lift on our glider. We wasted two years
because of that."

Turns out they built their 1900 and 1901 gliders usin'

arithmetic from a bunch of highfalutin' scientists. But the high-falutin' scientists didn't know beans about lift and thrust and all that other stuff. That's why the gliders didn't work good.

"So you got some NEW calculations?" I ask.

Mr. Orville nods his head. Over the winter, he tells me, he and Mr. Wilbur built themselves a wind tunnel, which is a box about the size of a coffin but with the ends open and a sheet of glass on top 'stead of wood so they could look inside. They stuck a big old fan at one end to blow air through the tunnel. Then they made a bunch of little wings in all different shapes and stuck 'em inside the tunnel to see what would happen when the wind hit 'em.

Wind is a funny thing, they say. It does different things to a square than it does to a rectangle. It does different things to a thin wing and a fat wing, a curved wing and a straight wing, a sharp edge and a round one. And it does different things dependin' on the speed of the wind too. They tested out just about every shape they could dream up.

"Will and I could hardly wait for morning to come to get at something that interested us," Mr. Orville says, his eyes all asparkle. "That's happiness!"

Spendin' the winter testin' out hunnerds of wing shapes to see which one flies the best didn't sound like happiness to ME. But I reckon testin' out hunnerds of lures to see which one catches the most bass most likely wouldn't be happiness to the Wrights, neither. Everybody's diffr'nt.

We finally get out to the campsite, and it is a MESS.

"It looks like a hurricane hit this place," Mr. Wilbur says.

"Well, that's cause a hurricane DID hit this place," I say.

Most fellers would of turned round right there and hightailed it back to where they come from. But nothin' doin'. Mr. Wilbur and Mr. Orville rolled up their sleeves and got to work.

August 31, 1902

Chloe Beasley sees me comin' up the road and says, are you still hangin' round them crazy dingbatters from Ohio who are buildin' the flyin' machine? I say, they ain't crazy, and Chloe says, they are too, cause anybody who thinks they can make a flyin' machine GOT to be crazy. I say, why don't you come on over to Kill Devil Hill and see for yourself if they're crazy? She says, she will NOT cause she got more important things to do than go look at some crazy dingbatters. Like what, I say, play with your durn dolls? She started in cryin' and I felt bad 'bout what I said.

September 1, 1902

We was hammerin' together the shed when we spot this feller in the distance comin' toward us. At first it looked like Captain Tate, but it turns out to be Dan Tate, his half brother, who looks a lot like the Captain. He ain't no spy, I know that for sure. Spies need to be right smart, and Dan Tate, well, he ain't clever enough to do no spyin', I'll just say that. But he's a good enough man, as men go.

Dan Tate tells the Wrights that Captain Tate and his family moved 15 miles up the beach. After kickin' the sand awhile, he asks Mr. Wilbur if he needed any help. For pay, that is.

Mr. Wilbur looks round the camp and hires Dan Tate on the spot as a carpenter and helper for 7 dollar a week.

There was no skeeters tormentin' us, which made things tolerable, and we four, includin' Dan Tate, set to work repairin' the shed. First we scooped the sand off the floor in buckets and toted it outside. Then we fixed the foundation and put on a new tar paper roof.

Mr. Wilbur and Mr. Orville was always lookin' to improve on things. They decided to make the shed longer this year so it would have a little kitchen and livin' room. To save space they put their sleepin' cots up in the rafters, hangin' from the roof. I told 'em, you might as well sleep in the air, cause that's where you spend your days.

Mr. Wilbur will eat just about any old thing, but Mr. Orville is particular about his grub. He stocked the little kitchen with canned tomatoes, eggs, peaches, biscuits, molasses, rice, and just about everything you'd ever want. He even penciled the date on each egg so he'd know which ones to eat first. That's how careful he is about things.

Mr. Orville loves milk, and there ain't no cows round here, so he sent me over to Kitty Hawk to buy powdered milk for him. You mix it with water, and it tastes like puke, if you ask me.

I was gonna take my bicycle into town, but Mr. Wilbur says to take his. It's black, with shiny silver trim. Turns out he built the bicycle special with gears set to ride on sand. I made it into Kitty Hawk in half an hour 'stead of an hour and a half like usual. Like I said, the Wrights are always lookin' to improve on things.

When I get back from the store with the milk, Mr. Orville has already fired up the stove. Now, I ain't never seen no real gasoline cookin' stove afore. You just set a match to the thing and it lights up like magic. You don't even have to keep addin' fuel.

Mr. Orville made some beef extract soup, but he says he has a cravin' for fowl. Dan Tate says, why don't you go out and shoot one of them scrawny chickens that are always runnin' round? Mr. Wilbur says no, but Mr. Orville says, that is a good idea. So he goes outside, and 5 minutes later we heard a BANG. Then he come back in with the chicken. Or what was left of it, anyways. By the time it was plucked and cooked, there weren't much meat left on it. It was hardly worth the bother, if you ask me.

While Mr. Orville was cookin', Mr. Wilbur went out and sunk a new well 6 or 8 feet down so they would have fresh water whenever they want it.

All in all, it was a cozy little home when we was done. Didn't have no electric, but it was nicer than my house, that was for sure. They even covered the wood chairs with burlap to make 'em soft to sit on.

They invited me to stay the night, but I promised mama I'd be home, so I took off as the sun was on its way down. I'm too wore out to write no more now. Next time I'll write about the mouse.

September 3, 1902

I said I was gonna write about the mouse, so now I'm gonna write about it.

While we was workin', this mouse was a-runnin' round the shed. A brown little critter. It didn't bother me none. Me and mama got lots of mice at home, and we don't pay 'em no mind. But Mr. Orville was tormented powerful by the critter. He would chase it round the little kitchen with a hammer, but the bugger always managed to escape through the cracks in the floorboards. Me and Dan Tate had a good laugh over it. Mr. Wilbur says that Mr. Orville has MUSOPHOBIA, which he says is a fear of mice. He even spelled it out for me so I'd get it right.

Anyways, the mouse weren't mommickin' nobody, but Mr. Orville decides he's gonna invent a mousetrap and capture the thing. Seemed to me he would be better off inventin' his flyin' machine and beatin' that Langley feller, but what do I know?

Mr. Orville took a whole afternoon and built a trap. It was a wondrous wooden thing with a steel spring that any respectable mouse would be proud to be caught in. Mr. Wilbur says the design is better'n their glider and they should put wings on the thing to see if IT will fly. I reckon that was a joke, but I never heard Mr. Wilbur joke afore, so I wasn't sure.

I told Mr. Orville that mice like to eat cornbread, so he

slipped a piece in for bait. Then we all sat round after supper waitin' for the critter to come to his last party.

Nothin' doin'. The little feller must of had a previous engagement. I knew he'd come soon, and I didn't want to miss the fun, so I asked Mr. Wilbur if I could sleep on the floor, and he says sure.

Afore we went to sleep, two interestin' things happened. First, Mr. Wilbur took his teeth right out of his mouth! Turns out he got busted up playin' hockey when he was 18, and he had to wear fake teeth ever since. Then I spied Mr. Orville rubbin' lemons all over his face. I say, what are you doin'? and he says the sun makes his skin dark, so he bleaches it with lemon juice. I never heard of a man bleaching his skin to look good, but I guess it takes all kinds.

Anyway, I sat round watchin' for the mouse a whit, but I got tuckered and fell asleep.

Then in the middle of the night I hear a SNAP, and we all wake up. Mr. Orville hops out of his bed and runs to check the trap. Empty. The little critter must of run off with the cornbread. Mr. Orville was plenty sore.

We go back to sleep, and not more than five minutes later Mr. Orville wakes up screaming.

"What is it, Orv?" Mr. Wilbur says, jumping up on his bed.

"The mouse ran over my FACE!" Mr. Orville shouts.

I had to laugh. How he managed not to let out a cuss word, I'll never know. Maybe he don't know no cuss words, is all I can figure, cause he was powerful sore.

"Maybe the mouse wanted to tell you he wants another piece of cornbread," Mr. Wilbur says, going back to sleep.

Well, Mr. Orville is so mommicked he can't sleep. He lights a lantern and picks up a piece of wood about a foot long.

"What are you gonna do with that?" I ask.

"Get revenge," Mr. Orville says.

"Go to sleep, Orv," says Mr. Wilbur.

"My mama told me it's bad luck to kill a mouse," I said.

"Especially for the mouse," says Mr. Orville.

So he is stalkin' round with his piece of wood, mouse hunting for a few minutes. Suddenly I spy the little feller in the corner, cute as a button, his eyes shining in the light of the lantern. Mr. Orville sees it too, and he chucks the wood at it. He misses, but he does hit something—a teacup that Dan Tate must of left on the floor. Pieces went flyin' all over.

"Orv, control yourself!" Mr. Wilbur says. But now Mr. Orville is REALLY mommicked. He grabs the shotgun from the rack and aims it at the spot in the corner where we seen the mouse last.

"For goodness sakes, Orv," says Mr. Wilbur. "It's just a little mouse!"

"It's going to be a little DEAD mouse," Mr. Orville says, without takin' his eye from the sight.

Sure enough, the critter pokes his little head out of that spot again and Mr. Orville mashes the trigger. BANG!

Well, I reckon he got it. Couldn't say for sure cause there was no body to speak of. Just some bits of fur and blood scattered acrost the floor. Anyways, that mouse didn't bother us or nobody else the rest of the night.

Don't that beat all?

September 8, 1902

Monday. With the buildin' done, Mr. Wilbur and Mr. Orville was finally fixin' to put together the new glider. That's right, GLIDER.

I say, "What are you buildin' another durn glider for? You DONE that already, TWICE now. You figured out in your wind tunnel back home all the right calculations. Let's get this show on the road! Put an engine on the thing and fly her. If you don't do it, that Langley feller will fly his machine first and grab the glory."

"Calm down," says Mr. Wilbur, who could prob'bly be calm even if he was standin' in the middle of a buffalo stampede. Nobody wants to fly the thing more than him and his brother, says he. But it's gonna be faster, cheaper, and safer if they make their mistakes on paper and with gliders than makin' 'em on an aeroplane with an engine and propellers and all. They are gonna test their new ideas before stickin' an engine on.

'Cordin' to Mr. Wilbur, once they learn how to fly the thing good and control it and all, it won't be no problem to buy an engine and propellers and fly it. That will be the easy part, he says.

I should of saved my breath to cool my coffee. Once these fellers come to a decision, there is no talkin' them out of it. So we started to build the durn glider.

September 15, 1902

Tween Mr. Wilbur, Mr. Orville, Dan Tate, and me workin' all at once, the new machine is comin' along, though Dan Tate does sometimes prefer jawin' to workin'.

This new glider will be bigger'n the last one, just like the last one was bigger'n the one afore it. The wings are thinner, but they're 32 foot from tip to tip, which is 10 foot more. The front rudder is 15 square foot. Mr. Orville says this machine has 305 square foot of wing surface area, and I don't know how a foot can be square anyway, so who am I to argue?

Mostly the new machine looks like the old one. It still got the hip cradle to control wing warpin'. But there's ONE big difference—now they got a TAIL on the thing. At the back of the glider is 2 fins, 6 foot high, stickin' up. Mr. Wilbur says he hopes it will make her easier to control. She looks more like a bird now.

Mr. Wilbur makes sure he weighs each little part afore he puts it on the glider, even the nails. He says the machine will weigh 120 pound exact when it's done.

At the end of the day, afore we attached the wings to the glider, we took 'em out and flew 'em as a kite. They flew real good. Then we put on the struts that was left over from last year's glider. She is nearly done.

September 19, 1902

We finally finished puttin' together the glider round noon. She come out to 120 pound, just like Mr. Wilbur said she would. She is a durn pretty bird. I asked if I could get the first ride, and Mr. Wilbur looked at me with that look that looked like he didn't want me askin' no more. Leastways till it's perfected.

Like always, they said they had to test her out afore they put a pilot on her. We attached ropes and brought the glider out of the shed. When a good wind come up, they let it pick the glider up and fly her as a kite, just to make certain she could take the wind without fallin' apart. They snapped a few photographs, I reckon in case the thing cracked up on the first glide, so they'd have something to remember her by.

Mr. Wilbur and Mr. Orville liked what they seen, cause they say, let's take the thing over to Little Hill and glide her. We did, and Mr. Wilbur climbed on board after we pointed her into the wind. Me and Mr. Orville each took a wing and ran with it. The glider lifted off nice and easy and coasted all the way down to the bottom, pretty as can be.

"Your turn, Orv," Mr. Wilbur says after we toted her back up the dune. Now, Mr. Orville ain't never flown afore, so far as I knew. But he climbed on board like he was born there, and when he gave the signal, we run her down the slope. He flew her just as pretty as his brother and landed her even a little furtherer. Me and Dan Tate let out a cheer.

They traded off after that, Mr. Wilbur makin' one glide and Mr. Orville the next. They was bein' careful at first, only flyin' a few foot off the ground, and sometimes only a few inches. Then they made a few gentle turns, testin' the wing warpin'. Mr. Orville says he thinks the tail rudder solved the problems they had last year.

All told, they made about 20 glides. On one of 'em a nice blow of wind come along as Mr. Wilbur was halfway down the hill. It lifted the glider up maybe ten foot, and it just hung her there in the air in one place without movin' forward or back. Like a picture hangin' on a wall. She just sat there on a gust of wind. It was a beautiful sight to see.

September 20, 1902

I got to the Wright camp early, and the glider was already in the air, coastin' down Big Hill like a feather. Looked to me like they could of stuck an engine on the thing and flown her forever, but Mr. Wilbur says they got a whole lot more testin' to do till they feel they got the thing perfected. But glide after glide looked plenty perfected to me.

Durin' lunch one of the surfmen comes over from the Kitty Hawk Life Saving Station and says a shipment come in at the wharf for the Wrights. Mr. Wilbur and Mr. Orville look at each other sort of glum like. I say, what is it and they say that their old friend Octave Chanute has made hisself a glider and asked 'em if he could test it at Kitty Hawk. Chanute and some other feller will be comin' down in 2 weeks.

"What do you want that old Chanute coot comin' round again

for?" I say. "All's he does is eat a gutful of your grub, take up space, and waste your time. He don't do a lick of work."

Mr. Wilbur says hush and Chanute is a great scientist, and besides, they feel sorry for the old guy cause his wife died in April after bein' married to him for 45 years. I say I can't believe she could stand him that long, and she prob'bly kilt herself. Mr. Wilbur says I better be on good behavior when Chanute gets here.

Seemed like a wise time to bring up somethin' I'd been a-thinkin' about for a long time. Mr. Wilbur and Mr. Orville are good, decent men. But they never mentioned no wives. Never talked about pretty gals like most men. Didn't seem to care about women.

I tried to think of ways to ask 'em. Like I could of said, "So, you fellers got wives back home in Ohio?" or "When you fellers gonna get hitched?" But sometimes you just get the feelin' that a feller don't want to talk about some things. So I keep my big mouth shut.

Me, I'm fixin' to have a big family someday. Only problem is there ain't no gals round here my age, so who am I gonna marry, that little squirt Chloe Beasley? I'll prob'bly have to go to the mainland to find a wife.

September 22, 1902

Rain for the second day in a row. One of Chanute's gliders arrived at the wharf. Mr. Wilbur and Dan Tate toted it across the sand to camp.

Couldn't do no flyin' anyway on account of the rain, so the Wrights made some 'justments in the wires to their glider. Now the wingtips are a few inches below the center. I went home after. It looks like it's gonna fair up tomorrow.

September 23, 1902

The sun finally broke through the clouds and it was perfect flyin' weather. Nice winds, but not too strong. Mr. Orville couldn't wait to get the glider into the air.

We hauled her out, and as soon as we got her off the hill, you could see the flyin' was good. Mr. Wilbur and Mr. Orville took turns, and most glides stayed up 10 or more seconds, goin' 200 foot or more. The controls was workin' good. After one glide I actually thought I saw Mr. Wilbur SMILE! Hard to believe. Should have took a photo of that.

For a change, they didn't waste a lot of time measurin' things and writin' everything down in their durn notebook. All they wanted to do was fly.

> Everything is so much more satisfactory that we now believe that the flying problem is really nearing its solution.

—**Wilbur Wright**

The better they flew, the worse Dan Tate liked it, cause he and me was the ones who had to tote the glider up the hill each time. After 70 glides we was tuckered. But Mr. Orville wanted one last go, so we toted the machine up the hill and chucked her off.

She looked good for a hunnerd foot or so, and then a wind picked up and the right wing begun to rise. The machine nosed up till it was pointin' almost straight up.

"TURN THE FRONT ELEVATOR DOWN, ORV!" Mr. Wilbur shouted.

But it was too late. I could see Mr. Orville workin' the control, but nothin' was happenin'. She just stopped climbin', hung there a whit, and fell back.

The whole thing happened in a few seconds. Next thing we knew, the machine dropped from 25 or 30 foot and hit the sand. The glider broke apart like a pile of dry twigs.

We all run over, dead sure Mr. Orville was dead. The forward elevator was wrecked, and junk was all over the sand.

But Mr. Orville was just sittin' there, brushin' bits of splintered wood off his jacket like they was flies. He weren't sore that he cracked up, but he WAS sore cause his pant leg was tore a whit. Me and Dan Tate had to laugh. Once he saw his brother was all right, Mr. Wilbur started pickin' up the pieces.

September 27, 1902

I half expected Mr. Wilbur and Mr. Orville would be fixin' to venture home after the crack up, but nothin' doin'. They was fixin' the glider, which weren't in such bad shape after all. I woulda helped, but I had me some fish to catch and I promised mama I'd bring home some money.

When I left Kill Devil, they weren't talkin' about the crack up. It was like it never happened. They was talkin' about the 70 glides they made AFORE the crack up. That is the way they are.

September 30, 1902

The machine was all fixed up like new, and it glided even better. We was totin' the machine up Big Hill when Mr. Wilbur spots a feller in the distance walkin' toward Kill Devil. He says it might be Chanute or Doc Spratt, who he was expectin'. I say it is prob'bly a spy. But it weren't neither.

Turns out the feller was Mr. Wilbur and Mr. Orville's older brother Lorin. Seems he decided to come out to North Carolina to see what his brothers was up to. Never told a soul he was comin'. The three Wrights was all huggin' like they ain't seen each other in years.

Mr. Wilbur and Mr. Orville took the afternoon off from flyin' to show Mr. Lorin round and built a bed for him to sleep in. Mr. Lorin seems like a regular feller. He even got hisself a wife and four kids. But he might could be a liar cause he says that back in Ohio he works as a bookkeeper. I know that a zookeeper is paid to keep an eye on animals. But I don't reckon nobody would pay no money to somebody just to keep an eye on some books.

Dan Tate figured we oughta leave the Wrights alone to talk

over old times or whatever, so I went a-fishin' the rest of the day.

October 2, 1902

Our old friend Doc Spratt arrived yesterday. First thing he says to me is, "How come firemen wear red suspenders?" I say I don't know, and he says they wear red suspenders to hold their pants up. I say, "But why do they have to be RED?" Doc Spratt says it's a joke. I didn't get it, but I laughed anyway so he wouldn't feel bad. It was good to see him.

Doc Spratt said he didn't wanna come back to the Banks this year cause he don't care for cold weather, but Mr. Wilbur and Mr. Orville asked him so nice he couldn't say no. With Doc Spratt, Mr. Lorin, and Dan Tate runnin' round the camp, it is like a honeybee hive.

Mr. Wilbur and Mr. Orville took the glider out to show Mr. Lorin how it worked. They made a heap of glides, and one from the top of Big Hill went the furtherest of all, nearbout 500 foot. I thought it would NEVER land. I reckon this big flyin' problem they always jaw about is solved, so far as I can tell.

But Mr. Wilbur weren't smilin'. His big forehead was all wrinkled up with worryation as usual, and he and Mr. Orville was talkin' real close afore they explained it to the rest of us.

Far as I can tell, every so often when they make a slow turn, the back slides sideways 'stead of bankin' nicely like birds do. So what, I say, so long as it flies right most of the time? But Mr. Wilbur says the machine ain't perfected till he can control it ALL of the time.

"The problem has to be in the vertical tail," Mr. Wilbur kept sayin'.

Sittin' outside the tent, they jawed about the problem over dinner, and after dinner too. Dan Tate and Mr. Lorin tossed in ideas, but the two of 'em know about as much about flyin' as a duck knows about spellin'.

Mr. Wilbur lit a fire and brewed up a pot of coffee, and he and Mr. Orville kept on jawin' after the others got tired of it and went to sleep. Mr. Orville sat there starin' into the fire with his arms folded in front of him. Mr. Wilbur sat back in his chair, his hands clasped behind his back and throwin' his legs out in front. Every now and again they would scribble something on a piece of paper and then chuck the paper into the fire.

They like to argue, these two. Mr. Wilbur would say his idea and Mr. Orville would say it made no sense. Then Mr. Orville would say HIS idea, and Mr. Wilbur would say IT made no sense.

Then they'd argue a whit, and the next thing I knew, the two of 'em totally switched sides! That's something, innit?

They'd be shoutin' at each other:

"'Tis."

"'Tisn't either."

"'Tis too."

"'Tis not."

Finally I had to venture home. When I left, they was still jawin' with each other. For all I know, they was goin' at it all night.

October 3, 1902

When I got back next mornin', everybody was just gettin' up. Mr. Orville's eyes was all puffy, and he says he was lyin' in bed all night thinkin' about the problem. Probably drunk too much coffee to sleep.

Even though he was wore out, he was all excited too. Over breakfast he says he thinks he figured it all out in the middle of the night. All they needed to do, says he, is put a hinge on the rear vertical rudder so it can move back and forth like a boat rudder moves. Then the pilot could turn the rudder to fight against the drag on the low wing. Or something like that, anyways. I didn't catch it all.

Well, Mr. Wilbur didn't call him a dummy or nothin', even though Mr. Orville is his little brother. He thought it over for a whit. Then he says he's afraid that things might could be too complicated if the pilot has to work another control.

Then he snapped his fingers. What if, he says, they hook up the rudder control with the wing warpin' control? Then you could move your hips in the hip cradle to twist the wings and turn the tail at the same time.

Well, the two of 'em ran out to work on the glider without sayin' another word. They didn't even clean up the breakfast dishes, which weren't like them.

They spent the whole day workin' on the glider to make the rear rudder move and to attach it to the hip cradle. There weren't no time to test it afore the sun went down, so we'll do that tomorrow.

October 4, 1902

Well, sure enough, the thing worked. We toted her up Big Hill and chucked her off with Mr. Wilbur at the controls. He started off nice and straight, then he made a slow turn to the right, and then he made a slow turn to the left. From the top of the hill I could see the rear rudder move to and fro. He landed her nice and easy on the sand nearbout 500 foot down.

Mr. Wilbur, he hops out of the glider and runs to Mr. Orville like they ain't seen each other in years. I never seen him so excited.

"All three axes of motion are under control!" says Mr. Wilbur. "Pitch is controlled by the forward elevator. Roll is controlled by wing warping. Yaw is controlled by the movable rudder."

"Gentlemen," says Mr. Orville, turnin' to me and Doc Spratt and Dan Tate and Mr. Lorin, "I believe at long last we have discovered the secret of flight."

From the wind swept top of a Kill Devil Hill one hundred and twenty feet above the ground, a daring young aeronaut leaps into space and travelling upon a frail machine reaches the ground in safety hundreds of yards from whence he leaped. Next summer he will attach an electric motor and propeller to his contraption and vie with the birds in flight, defying gravity and adverse winds.

—*Elizabeth City Weekly Tar Heel,* **October 3, 1902**

October 5, 1902

Sunday. No flyin', of course. I done some fishin' and rode over to the Wright camp just to see what's what. Doc Spratt and Dan Tate wasn't round, so it was just the three Wright brothers sittin' outside the shed jawin'. Mr. Lorin clammed up when I come near, but Mr. Wilbur says it's okay to talk in front of me. Mr. Lorin whispers anyway.

"If you have truly solved the problem of human flight," he tells his brothers, "you'll go down in history with Alexander Graham Bell for his invention of the telephone, with Thomas Edison for his invention of the lightbulb. This could be the most important discovery in the history of mankind. You could be millionaires many times over if you play your cards right."

"We didn't enter into this for fame or fortune," Mr. Orville says.

"But you deserve them!" Mr. Lorin says. "You invested a lot

of time, a lot of money. You even risked your lives. Don't you deserve both credit and compensation for what you've accomplished? How would you feel if somebody came along, took your ideas, and made a fortune from them?"

Mr. Wilbur and Mr. Orville sat there, thinkin' it over.

"That's what I been tryin' to tell 'em all along," I say. "There are spies nosin' round everywhere."

"The flying problem still isn't completely solved," Mr. Wilbur says. "We have only glided. We need to make a sustained powered flight from level ground to prove human flight is practical."

"Sure, sure," Mr. Lorin says, "but you need to patent these discoveries right away, before Professor Langley or somebody else beats you to it. Now it is time for you to be thinking as businessmen, not just as inventors."

By that time Dan Tate and Doc Spratt come back, and they got company with 'em. It was that old Chanute coot who was here last year and some younger feller from Georgia who goes by the name Augustus Herring. The Herring feller was thin, with slicked back hair. Chanute says Herring is a famous aviator who used to work for Langley, but I ain't never heard of him.

Chanute and Herring show up with a big cart full of wood and supplies. Turns out Herring designed a glider of his own to test out. All they got to do is put it together.

If it was me, I woulda sent 'em packin'. The Wrights didn't need no distractions. But Mr. Wilbur and Mr. Orville was all polite, 'specially since Chanute's wife up and died only in April.

The surfmen from the lifesavin' station sent over a mess of bluefish. As we fixed dinner the men got to jabberin' about wind resistance and angle of attack and lift and drag and such. Soon as I could, I pull Mr. Orville aside.

"That Herring feller looks like a spy to me," I say.

"Johnny, if I had a nickel for every time you said somebody was a spy, I'd be a rich man," he says. "If he was here to spy on us, I don't think he would bring his own glider with him."

Still, I didn't trust Herring, and I don't reckon the Wrights did neither. Over dinner, I notice, Mr. Wilbur and Mr. Orville didn't happen to mention to anybody that just yesterday they SOLVED THE FLYIN' PROBLEM and made THE MOST IMPORTANT DISCOVERY IN THE HISTORY OF MANKIND.

Of course, Mr. Wilbur and Mr. Orville ain't braggarts. But I reckon they don't want Herring or Chanute stealin' their secrets, neither. Maybe they finally smarted up.

After dinner Mr. Orville pulls out his mandolin and Mr. Wilbur plays his harmonica as the sun goes down. They should stick with flyin', if you ask me. I left in the middle of Home on the Range.

October 6, 1902

We spent the whole durn day puttin' Herring's glider together, only he don't call it no glider, he calls it a MULTI-WING cause it got 5 wings stacked on top of each other. I s'pose he figures five wings will give him five times as much lift as one wing.

Everybody helped. Me, Dan Tate, Doc Spratt, Mr. Lorin, Mr. Orville, Mr. Wilbur. The Wrights didn't take their glider out of the shed all day, like they didn't want nobody to see it. While we all hammered and nailed, that old coot Chanute stood round mostly, a-flappin' his gums about how glorious the world'll be after the aeroplane is perfected.

Herring walked round tellin' everybody what to do, actin' like he was the biggest dog in the meat house. His glider don't have no wing warpin' or rudder or nothin'. Just a catawampus mess of wings and a tail. It was sorry lookin', if you ask me.

The two of us was alone for a minute, and I ask him how come he ain't got no control system on his machine.

"The Wrights talk only of rudders and elevators and control system nonsense," he says. "The first man to get off the ground for a few seconds with an engine will be known forever as the inventor of the aeroplane. And that man will be ME."

I got sick of him real fast, and I hope his glider don't fly a foot.

Several things I had heard about Mr. Herring's relations with Mr. Langley and yourself seemed to me to indicate that he might be of a somewhat jealous disposition, and possibly inclined to claim for himself rather more credit than those with whom he might be working would be willing to allow.

—Wilbur Wright, in a letter to Octave Chanute, September 5, 1902

October 7, 1902

Well, the baseball season is over. My Cubs won 68 games and lost 69 and finished in 5th place. A little better, I reckon, but nothin' to brag on. They say there's gonna be a World Serious next year. Don't look like the Cubs have a chance to be in it, even with Chance and Tinker in the infield.

October 8, 1902

We took Herring's multiwing out for a test. What a joke! The first ten tries that thing wouldn't even heist off the sand. Me and Doc Spratt was doin' all we could not to laugh. "Perhaps you should consider removing a wing or two," Mr. Orville says to Herring.

Herring didn't have to. The thing finally gets a few feet in the air, and then it hits the dune and three of the durn wings fall off all by themselves! I reckon it flew 20 foot at best.

Doc Spratt was doubled over laughing. Herring looked mad as a stuck pig. He says we didn't launch her right, but the truth is I seen fish that could fly bettern his multiwing.

We picked up the pieces and toted the junk back to camp to fix Herring's machine. I can't believe Mr. Wilbur and Mr. Orville are wastin' their time with somebody else's glider. If it was me, I would of kicked Chanute and Herring and their multiwing out of here by now.

While we was fixin' Herring's machine, old Chanute says to Mr. Wilbur, so, when are we gonna test YOUR new machine? Mr. Wilbur looks like he was hopin' nobody would ask, and says, maybe tomorrow if the wind is right.

October 10, 1902

Herring's multiwing is fixed, so we took it out for another go. It was pitiful. Doc Spratt whispered to me that that turkey wouldn't fly if you attatched a hot air balloon to it. Herring says the problem is the wind ain't right. I say his HEAD ain't right. Herring is all highfalutin.

That old coot Chanute kept pesterin' Mr. Wilbur and Mr. Orville to take out THEIR glider, and I reckon they finally did it just to shut the old gasbag up. We pulled the glider out and toted it up Big Hill. The wind was blowin' harder from the northeast, but it didn't seem to trouble the Wrights none. Mr. Orville clum on. Me and Mr. Wilbur each grabs a wing and runs.

The glider lifts off pretty as a picture. A little wind come up

and holds it in the air. Mr. Orville dipped the wings left and right before landin' soft in the sand nearbout 500 foot away. Mr. Lorin made some photographs.

I wish I had a photograph of Herring's face while Mr. Orville was up in the air. He looked powerful sore. After the glider was down and we fetched it, Herring was walkin' round the machine and lookin' it over real careful. If that jaybird ain't a spy, I don't know who is.

October 11, 1902

Herring says he wants to test his durn multiwing one more time. Mr. Wilbur says, maybe you should try flyin' it as a kite. Herring is all insulted and says his machine ain't no child's toy. But even old Chanute says it's a good idea, so Herring says okay.

Well, the thing wouldn't even fly as a durn KITE. The wind was bendin' the wings so bad they nearbout broke. Mr. Orville tells Herring he don't think the multiwing is AIRWORTHY, whatever that means, and Herring gets all sore.

"You stole my ideas!" he says, pointin' at the Wrights.

"And what ideas did you have?" says Mr. Wilbur.

Old Chanute tries to calm Herring down, but he storms down the beach all mad.

After Herring is out of earshot, Doc Spratt says, "If he is an honest man, he ought to sue his face for slander." I didn't know what slander was, but it sounded comical, so I laughed along with the others.

October 14, 1902

Mr. Lorin had to venture back to his wife and kids in Ohio, so Mr. Wilbur and Mr. Orville took him to Kitty Hawk to see him off at the wharf. Dan Tate went with 'em.

Old Chanute says he's gonna take a walk down the beach to birdwatch. I didn't want to hang round camp with Herring, so I decide to go a-fishin'.

I get about a mile on my bicycle when I remembered that I left my fishhooks back at the Wright camp. So I turn round and head back.

I thought the fishhooks was in the shed, where the glider was at, so I go in there to get 'em. Soon as I go in, I hear a noise on the other side of the glider. I look up and it's Herring. He acts like he's doin' nothin', but it looks to me like he was hidin' so I wouldn't see him.

"What are YOU doin' here?" I say.

"That is none of your business, boy."

I seen he's holdin' something in his hand. He slips it behind his back, but I see it's one of them newfangled Kodak Brownie cameras. Chloe Beasley's mama got one too. After you take your photographs, you mail the camera to Kodak and they send your pictures back, along with the camera loaded with new film.

"What are you takin' photographs of?" I say to Herring.

"The Wright brothers stole my ideas for human flight," he says. "I am merely gathering photographic evidence so I will have proof when I take them to court. It would be wise, for your sake, young man, to keep this to yourself. You could be SUPEENUD."

I didn't know what supeenud meant, but it sounded like it might hurt. I grabbed up my fishhooks and got out of there. I went a-fishin' for the rest of the day.

Me, I don't believe a word of what Herring said. There's no way Mr. Wilbur and Mr. Orville was spyin' on Herring. They are so goody-goody they wouldn't a known how to tell a lie to save their lives.

All afternoon I was ponderin' should I tell Mr. Wilbur and Mr. Orville what I saw. If I DON'T tell 'em, that wampus cat Herring might use his photographs to build a flyin' machine just like theirs and win the race for the sky. And if I DO tell 'em, who knows what Herring might do? He might kill 'em for all I know. He might kill ME too.

I was mommicked.

October 15, 1902

When I go back to Kill Devil, old Chanute and Herring are packin' up their stuff to venture home. Chanute says they gotta hurry or they will miss their boat to Washington. Herring shoots me a look so I know he remembers what happened yesterday.

"Gentlemen," old Chanute says to the Wrights, "I wish I could be a witness when you conquer the air, as I believe you will shortly do. But we must take our leave. In appreciation of your hospitality, Mr. Herring and I have decided to give you the multi-wing glider as a gift."

Some GIFT! That's like bringin' your trash over to somebody's house and leavin' it there for THEM to throw away. Any normal man would of frapped him, but Mr. Wilbur and Mr. Orville just bowed and acted like it was the best present they ever got. They all shook hands, and Dan Tate took old Chanute and that scoundrel Herring to the wharf.

"Mr. Wilbur," I say after Chanute and Herring are out of earshot, "I believe that Herring feller was a-spyin' on you."

"Johnny, this time I believe you are right," agrees Mr. Orville.

"You think he's gonna go build his own flyin' machine just like yours?"

"It is entirely possible," says Mr. Wilbur.

"Either that, or Mr. Herring is going to Washington to try and sell our secrets to Professor Langley," says Mr. Orville.

Some men would of stopped Herring in his tracks. Some men might of shot him dead in the sand afore he got to the wharf. But that weren't the Wrights nature. All they wanted to do was get back to work.

> Before he left camp in 1902 we foresaw and predicted the object of his visit to Washington; we also felt certain that he was making a frenzied attempt to mount a motor on a copy of our 1902 glider and thus anticipate us.

—**Wilbur Wright**

October 18, 1902

The supplies are gettin' low at the Wright camp. They are down to eatin' mostly beans. I brought 'em some bluefish I caught to cheer 'em up, but I didn't have to. With that old coot Chanute and that thievin' spy Herring gone, Mr. Wilbur and Mr. Orville looked happier than pigs in a mud puddle.

Me and Dan Tate and Doc Spratt helped bring the glider out to Big Hill, and the Wrights were in the air most all day. The wind got up to 30 mile per hour and she handled just fine. They was glidin' 500 foot easy, makin' turns, and hoverin' in one place for nearbout a minute.

Every so often the glider would touch the ground wing first and spin round in a circle. Mr. Wilbur called it "well diggin'." But mostly, they'd land her so gentle they could bring her to a runnin' stop with their feet touchin' the ground 'stead of the skids.

With that hard wind it was easier to tote the glider back up the hill over and over. We'd just angle the wings a whit and let the wind do the work. I worked up the courage to ask for a ride again, but nothin' doin'. "Not yet, Johnny," says Mr. Wilbur.

After lunch Mr. Wilbur and Mr. Orville had a contest to see who could make the longest glide. Mr. Wilbur won: 622 foot in 26 seconds!

We spied a steamer out in Albemarle Sound. It started comin' in close to shore for no good reason but to see what the Wrights was up to. Mr. Wilbur says it's time to stop flyin' for the day. Looks like he finally smarted up about spies.

I got them more fish to eat, and Mr. Orville cooked it up. While we ate, they started talkin' about their NEXT machine. They don't call it a glider no more. It'll be a real AEROPLANE. They already figured out the size of the wings and propellers, how much pounds the engine and frame will weigh, and how much horsepower they need to get off the ground and stay off the ground.

"Hurry up!" I say. "Put an engine on it NOW afore that no good spy Herring gets HIS aeroplane into the air!"

But the Wrights just can't be hurried nohow. They say they will come back next year after they spend all winter designin' their new machine. Sometimes you just can't talk sense to people.

October 19, 1902

The beans is all gone. Mr. Orville told me he had a spoonful of milk powder for breakfast. It's gettin' cold, too. They had to run a fire all night to keep warm.

Dan Tate had to light out for a fishin' trip, and Doc Spratt had to venture home. We took Doc to the Kitty Hawk wharf, and there was a telegram addressed to Mr. Wilbur waitin' at the lifesaving station. It said SMITHSONIAN INSTITUTION on it.

"Well, what do you know," Mr. Wilbur says, "it's from Professor Samuel Langley!"

"What's he want?" I say, tryin' to peek at the words.

"The professor asks if he can have permission to visit Kitty Hawk and witness our experiments."

Mr. Wilbur crumpled up the telegram and chucked it into the fireplace.

Mr. Orville says, "It looks like our friend Mr. Herring has been talking with Professor Langley."

October 23, 1902

When I got to Kill Devil, the Wrights already packed up the glider in the rafters of the shed. They put Herring's multiwing in storage too.

We did a little birdwatchin' in the woods, then walked off down the beach a ways. They picked up some starfish, shells, and king crabs to bring home as souvenirs for their nieces and nephews in Ohio. They're fixin' to venture home tomorrow.

"You can't light out NOW," I say one last time. "If Herring told Langley everything he knows, he might could copy your machine and get it in the air next week."

Mr. Wilbur just shrugs. All he says is, "An honest man is at the mercy of a hostile world."

October 28, 1902

The Wrights left camp early in the mornin'. It was a cold drizzle as I walked the four miles to Kitty Hawk with 'em.

"What are you gonna do if that Langley feller beats you?" I say before they get on the boat to Elizabeth City.

"I'll shake his hand and congratulate him," says Mr. Wilbur. "Every race has a winner and a loser."

"If we are the losers, there are always a lot of bicycles in Ohio that need fixing," says Mr. Orville.

They get on the boat and wave good-bye. As it pulls away Mr. Orville shouts to me, "Next year we'll fly."

We are thinking of building a machine
next year with 500 square ft surface. . . .
If all goes well the next step will be to
apply a motor.

—Wilbur Wright, in a letter to George Spratt, December 1902

Book 4: 1903
TWELVE SECONDS

We are going to have the chance to learn
a whole lot of things when we get to
Kitty Hawk this year, maybe very much to
our sorrow.

—Orville Wright, June 7, 1903

March 6, 1903

Happy birthday to ME. I am 18 years old today which means I can durn well do whatever I please and nobody can stop me. So I say to myself, what do I want to do, anyhow? I tell mama, I want to go see a motion picture show, cause I ain't have never seen one. And you can't stop me. Mama says, go ahead, see if I care, but they won't let you into the motion picture theater without shoes.

I didn't wanna go by myself, and Elijah Baum didn't wanna go. Mama says why don't you take Chloe Beasley? And I say, I don't want to go to no motion picture with that squirt.

So go by yourself, mama says.

March 7, 1903

Me and Chloe Beasley went to the fancy theater in Nags Head, where they was were playin' this new motion picture called The Great Train Robbery. It was made by the great Thomas Alva Edison hisself. It is the longest motion picture ever made—12 minutes! There was a lot of shootin' and chasin', and Chloe nearbout jumped out of her seat cause it looked like those train robbers was were gonna come right out of the screen and shoot US too.

After, I got Chloe ice cream and Elijah Baum saw us. He started in razzing me cause he ain't never seen me with shoes on, and he was sayin' me and Chloe might as well get married. I frapped him one and he shut his mouth.

April 20, 1903

Baseball started up again, and there is definitely going to be a World Serious at the end of this season. The Cubs picked up this new second baseman name of Johnny Evers who is s'posed to be a marvel at turning the double play. Maybe with Tinker and Evers and Chance in the infield, they ~~got~~ have a chance.

I had a dream last night. There is this aeroplane flying round and round over Kill Devil Hill, making lazy circles. Finally she lands, and I run over to say howdy to Mr. Wilbur and Mr. Orville. Only they ~~ain't~~ aren't IN the aeroplane. An old feller gets out and says his name is Professor Samuel Langley. Don't that beat all?

July 14, 1903

I looked at the newspaper to see how my Cubs were doing. They're in third place behind the New York Giants. But more important, I see this:

LANGLEY'S NEW AERODROME.

Scientists Working Hard to Complete It—Houseboat Ready to Move It from Washington.

WASHINGTON, July 12.—Scientists working under the direction of Prof. Langley, Secretary of the Smithsonian Institution, are working incessantly to complete the aerodrome devised by Prof. Langley, so that practical tests may be made, but thus far it is uncertain when these tests will take place. Prof. Langley has been out of

That Langley feller is getting close to flying, and there's no sign of Mr. Wilbur and Mr. Orville. I am afraid they are about to lose the race.

August 8, 1903

Chloe Beasley turned 8 years old today, so I dropped off some mackerel for her and her mama to eat. Chloe says she ~~ain't~~ isn't going to school ~~no~~ anymore. Her mama needs help at home. I said you better learn to read first before you stop going to school. And she says she ~~don't~~ doesn't need to learn how to read. There's no talking sense to her.

Chloe, she says she is catching up to me in age, and I say, no, you ~~ain't~~ aren't, you are still ten years younger'n me and always will be. Chloe says that's so, but when she is 20 I will be 30 and that won't be such a differn'ce. And when she is 50 and I am 60 that won't hardly be no differn'ce at all cause we'll just be 2 old people. So little by little she is catching up to me, she says.

She maybe can't read, but she is good at arithmetic. I say you think you're so smart just cause your 8 now, but you won't catch up to me till I'm 10 years dead.

August 10, 1903

Langley FLEW! It said so right in the newspaper. Well, it was only a 6 foot model, and it didn't have no pilot, but it had an engine and propeller. The newspaper says it flew for 30 second and 1,500 foot. I reckon Langley is gonna win the race. Still no sign of Mr. Wilbur nor Mr. Orville.

The Cubs are still in third place behind the Giants. Looks like it ~~ain't~~ isn't gonna happen for 'em this year, like usual.

August 30, 1903

Langley is gonna try to fly a real aeroplane next week. It says so right in the newspaper.

Langley's Aerodrome Not Damaged.

WIDEWATER, Va., Aug. 29.—Prof. Manley stated to-day that no damage had been done to Prof. Langley's aerodrome in the storm last night. He said the inventor would remain down the river, indicating that with good weather conditions a launching will be attempted early next week. The sunken naphtha launch and the float were recovered to-day. The boat was not greatly damaged.

September 7, 1903

Didn't see nothin' in the newspaper about Langley. I don't know if he flew or not.

September 20, 1903

Finally I see somethin' about Langley.

LANGLEY WANTS MORE MONEY.

Explains Necessities of Aerial Navigation to Army Fortifications Board.

Special to The New York Times.

WASHINGTON, Sept. 19.—The Army Board of Ordnance and Fortifications is taking lessons in aeronautics in connection with Prof. Langley's flying machine experiments.

The board appropriates for the Langley airship. Congress, in the Fortifications act of June 6, 1902, allowed the board $100,000 to make tests with a view to the utilization by the Government of the most effective guns, small arms, projectiles, torpedoes,

The newspaper says "a further allowance of money is absolutely indispensable to the complete execution of his experiments." I don't know what that means, but I reckon one thing for dead sure: Langley ~~ain't~~ hasn't flown yet.

September 23, 1903

It's gettin' near the end of September, and I was deadset sure those Wright brothers ~~ain't~~ ~~aren't~~ weren't a-comin' this year if they weren't here by now. It's gettin' airish out, and soon it'll be too cold for 'em to fly.

But then, I get word from Elijah Baum in Kitty Hawk—a boatful of aeroplane parts arrived at the wharf yesterday. I knew it had to be them.

September 25, 1903

My Cubs are getting better! They finished the season at 82-56. Third place ~~ain't~~ isn't half bad. Course, it isn't half good, neither.

September 26, 1903

Mr. Wilbur and Mr. Orville showed up at Kitty Hawk round noon. They were powerful happy to see me. I'm taller'n Mr. Wilbur now, and he says he is fixing to put me to work and use my new muscles.

Mr. Wilbur says they applied for a patent on their flying machine in March, but the government turned 'em down. I tell 'em what I heard about Langley, but they know it already. Mr. Wilbur says Langley is s'posed to make an attempt in a week or two. Mr. Wilbur and Mr. Orville say they will make a try as soon as they build their new machine. Then they'll be going home to Ohio in time for Christmas, whether they fly or not.

We walk out to the old campsite, and it's wrecked, like usual. We got so much rain this summer that it nearbout turned into a lake. The Wrights don't seem mommicked. They're fixing to fix the shed—which they now call THE SUMMER HOUSE—and build another one to use as a workshop and aeroplane hangar. They hired Dan Tate as a helper, and Doc Spratt will be coming down shortly too.

> The hills are in the best shape for gliding they have ever been, and things are starting off more favorably than in any year before.

—Orville Wright

September 28, 1903

The wind was just right for flying, so we stopped fixing the summer house and pulled last year's glider out of storage. She still flies like a bird, and Mr. Orville had her up for 30 second on one glide. She was beautiful hanging in the sky.

In the afternoon we finished fixing the summer house and started building the hangar for the aeroplane. At the end of the day we ~~was~~ were tired as a hound after a long chase. Dan Tate wanted to go on home, and he got sore when Mr. Wilbur asked him to clean the supper dishes.

"Why can't the boy clean the dishes?" he says.

"We're paying YOU," Mr. Wilbur says, "not the boy."

"I ain't no boy," I say, "but I'll clean the dishes if you want."

That seemed tolerable to everybody, so Dan Tate went home and I ~~done~~ did the dishes.

September 29, 1903

The hangar ~~ain't~~ isn't done, but we started building The Flyer anyhow. That's what they call it. THE FLYER. Seemed to me they could of just put an engine on the glider and flew her. But Mr. Wilbur says the frame got to be stronger on account of the weight of the engine. The balance is diffr'nt too. He knows better'n me, I figure.

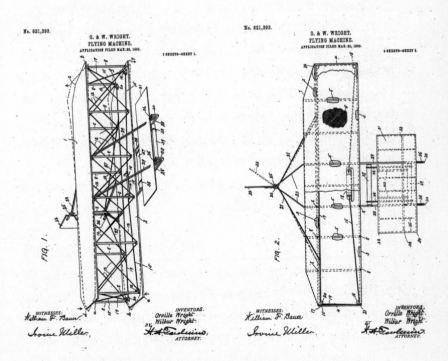

Mr. Orville unrolled the blueprint for the big whopper flying machine on the table. The wingspan will be 40 foot and there's 6 foot, 'tween the 2 wings. Put together, it's 520 square foot of wing. This baby is bigger than anything they built before.

"It's simple, really," Mr. Orville says to me as he shows me the blueprint. "The fuel in the engine is combusted, pushing pistons to turn a crankshaft, which through a series of chains turns the propellers. These rotate with enough thrust to move the machine forward. At a certain speed, the airflow across the wings creates upward pressure, and when it is greater than the weight of the machine, the machine lifts off the ground."

Simple to him, maybe. The important thing, Mr. Wilbur says, is the weight. Back home in Ohio they figured out The Flyer couldn't be no more'n 625 pounds and get off the ground. That's including the engine and pilot. Mr. Wilbur and Mr. Orville both weigh near 140. They know The Flyer is near 290 cause they weighed all the pieces back in Ohio. So the engine, propellers, and transmission got to be less than 200 pounds. They worked out all the arithmetic and everything.

"Of course," Mr. Orville says, "one good crack up and we will have 485 pounds of junk."

October 2, 1903

It is getting colder than an old maid's kisses. The water in the washbasin was froze up in the morning. Mr. Wilbur and Mr. Orville like to build when the weather is bad, but soon as it is nice and the wind is right, they pull out the glider and fly her.

The hangar is finished. This afternoon we built THE GRAND JUNCTION RAILROAD. That's what Mr. Orville calls the takeoff rail The Flyer will set upon. See, this machine is too durn heavy to tote up a sand dune. They got to launch her from level ground. So they got some long 2 by 4s and covered 'em with a thin metal strip to make the rail.

Put together, it's 60 foot long. The aeroplane is gonna slide along the rail on a wooden truck that has metal rollers. Then, when she lifts off the takeoff rail, the truck stays on the ground.

I say, why don't you just put WHEELS on her instead? Mr. Wilbur says wheels would add weight, and besides, they wouldn't roll good on sand. I swear, these Wright boys think of everything. I'm starting to think this thing might could really fly.

October 7, 1903

It looked like we ~~was~~ were in for some weather, so I rode over to the Kitty Hawk Life Saving Station to check the telegraph wire. Turns out there was a newspaper just in from Washington. They got big letters on the front page that say . . .

FLYING MACHINE FIASCO

Prof. Langley's Airship Proves a Complete Failure.

I ride over to the Wright camp so fast I can't hardly breathe when I get there. I just hand 'em the newspaper, and Mr. Orville reads it.

Prof. Manley, in the Car of the Aero-drome, Escapes with a Ducking in the Potomac.

WIDEWATER, Va., Oct. 7.—The sixty-foot steel-built flying machine, the climax of years of exhaustive study in the efforts of Prof. Samuel P. Langley, Secretary of the Smithsonian Institution, to solve the problem of mechanical flight in mid-air, was launched to-day, and the experiment, carefully planned and delayed for months, proved a complete failure. The immense airship sped rapidly along its seventy-foot track, was carried by its own momentum for 100 yards, and then fell gradually into the Potomac River, whence it emerged a total wreck.

Seems Langley tried to launch a 750 pound flying machine from a boat in the Potomac River near Washington. The wings broke up before it left the launch, and the thing dumped into the river. Langley was even too chicken to be the pilot. He hired some other feller named Manley to do it, and the feller was lucky to get out of the wreck alive.

Mr. Wilbur and Mr. Orville didn't stand up and cheer or ~~nothing~~ anything. All they said was they were glad they ~~ain't~~ don't ~~got~~ have ~~no~~ any newspaper reporters followin' THEM round to write articles when THEY crack up.

"So I guess you don't have to worry about that Langley feller ~~no~~ any more," I say.

Mr. Orville looks down to the bottom of the newspaper and reads out loud, "PROFESSOR LANGLEY HOPES TO MAKE ANOTHER ATTEMPT AT HUMAN FLIGHT BEFORE CHRISTMAS."

"So do we," says Mr. Wilbur.

October 8, 1903

If I die and you found this, you'll know what happened.

It was 2 P.M. We ~~was~~ were unpacking parts of The Flyer when dark clouds roll in, and quick as you can snap a finger, the wind breezes up and the clouds open. I seen some rain before, but not like this. I never knew heaven had so much water in it. Dan Tate lit out for home quick before it got bad. Me, I wasn't going nowhere.

The floor was underwater in an hour. The wind must of been 75 miles per hour, and we couldn't hardly hear each other talk. Mr. Wilbur was afraid parts of The Flyer might blow away cause the hangar was not done yet. I was afraid we was all gonna be drownded.

We put braces inside the summer house so it wouldn't blow down. It kept raining, and Mr. Wilbur says I should sleep over. No fooling! If I tried to ride home, I'da been blown into the ocean.

Couldn't sleep anyway with the wind and rain. Round 4 A.M. a corner of the roof gave way. Mr. Orville put on an overcoat and clum up on a ladder outside to nail down the rest before the whole roof blew off. He put the nails in the coat pocket, but he couldn't get at 'em cause the coat was flapping in the wind. Finally it went over his head. It would of been comical if we didn't all think we was gonna die.

Mr. Orville put the nails in his mouth so he could get at 'em easy, but the wind was so hard it blew his arm as it come down on the nail, and he mashed his fingers a few times before he got the roof nailed down.

We are all soaked to the bone. The storm looks like it's dyin' down now, so I'm gonna try to sleep.

October 9, 1903

I went out to the top of Big Hill and could see all the trees and chimneys and telegraph lines knocked down by the storm. I hear tell five boats washed ashore tween Kitty Hawk and Cape Hatteras. A few of 'em I could see from the top of the dune. Elijah Baum told me the body of one of the captains washed up near Kitty Hawk, but that may just be one of his stories.

I rode home to check on mama and the Beasleys and other folks I know, and they are all right.

The only good news is a heap of mullet were sighted up the beach at Corolla. That's good news for the fishermen, like me and Dan Tate, who come back after the storm.

Mr. Wilbur and Mr. Orville repaired the damage to the shed and even tried a few glides in the afternoon. On Mr. Orville's second glide a gust come along and threw him down so hard the left wing brushed Mr. Wilbur on the head. He had a headache the rest of the day.

October 12, 1903

We put together three sections of the upper wing. On this new Flyer, only the back edges of the wings warp, 'stead of the whole wing. But just like on the glider, the pilot warps the wings and the rudder moves all by itself.

Mr. Wilbur tells me to go measure the wings. I do, and I run over to him all mommicked cause the right wing is 4 inches LONGER than the left! He says they did that on purpose on account of the engine will be mounted a little to one side and it's got to balance. These Wright boys think of everything.

October 14, 1903

We stretched the cloth over the wings. This time the bottoms of the wings are covered with cloth just like the tops.

The World Serious is over, and the Boston Pilgrims beat the Pittsburgh Pirates five games to three. Next year, Cubs all the way!

October 15, 1903

We finished the lower wings. Nobody is talking about Langley, but I am thinking about him. We know he is gonna try to fly again soon. I am working extra fast to finish building The Flyer so they can fly the durn thing before Langley flies his. But Mr. Wilbur and Mr. Orville want everything just so. Every nail and screw has got to be right, or they pull it out and start again. I wish they'd hurry up.

October 17, 1903

We put together the elevator, tail, skids, braces, wires, pulleys, and uprights.

October 19, 1903

The frame is nearbout done, but the wind was just right for

flying, so they pulled out the glider and spent the afternoon in the air. Mr. Orville got her all the way up to 50 foot or so off the sand, and he kept her up there a full minute. He landed 603 foot away from the top of Big Hill.

They're setting all kinds of records for gliding, but they don't look to be in any big rush to make history. You ask me, they should get the engine on The Flyer and forget about all this gliding. I keep tellin' 'em, "Hurry up, cause Langley's gonna beat you," but they say safety is more important. They wanna be the first to fly, but they ain't aren't willing to die to be the first to fly.

October 23, 1903

Doc Spratt arrived this morning with some new jokes from the mainland. We told him all about the big storm he was lucky to miss, but the Doc ain't isn't happy cause now it's getting cold, and if there's one thing Doc Spratt don't doesn't like, it's cold. So we covered the walls of the summer house with carpet to keep out drafts.

Mr. Orville made a heating stove out of the old gas can to warm up the place. It worked tolerably, but the thing threw off so much soot and smoke we had to sit on the floor so we wouldn't choke. Mr. Orville found some pipe and vented the stove outside, which helped some.

Even with the stove running, Doc Spratt says it was cold as the North Pole in there. Mr. Wilbur says he don't doesn't need no thermometer to tell how cold it is. He just counts how many blankets he needs to sleep under. If it's a 1 blanket night, it ain't isn't so cold. 2 blankets and it's getting airish. A 3 blanket night and it's durn cold. Last night was a 5 blanket and 2 quilt night.

Dan Tate ~~ain't~~ isn't happy. The price of fish went up after the storm, so he says he wants a raise or he's gonna go fishing instead of working for the Wrights. Mr. Wilbur says he'll give Dan a raise, but only if he puts in ten hours of work each day. They shake on it, but Dan Tate still didn't look too happy.

October 28, 1903

Wednesday. Dan Tate up and quit! What happened was Mr. Wilbur asked him to go out and collect driftwood for the stove, and Dan didn't want to. He tells Mr. Wilbur he can BUY wood for just 3 dollar a cord in town, so why bother running up and down the beach to find it? Mr. Wilbur says we are paying you to work. Dan Tate didn't like that, so he just took his hat and walked out!

Don't need him anyhow. The frame is done. Me and Doc Spratt and the Wrights can do the rest. Dan Tate will miss out and be sorry he left when we fly this thing.

November 2, 1903

It's time to put the engine on The Flyer, and it's about time, I say! All summer Mr. Wilbur and Mr. Orville wrote to a bunch of companies that make engines, but none of 'em could build what they asked for. So they did what they always do. They designed their OWN durn engine, and a feller named Charley Taylor who works in their bicycle shop built it. The engine finally showed up at Kitty Hawk wharf, and we toted it over to camp.

I worked on a fishing boat for a whit, so I know a thing or two about engines. This one is a beaut. The crankcase is aluminum, and the crankshaft is made of high carbon tool steel. It's got 4 cast iron in-line cylinders with a 4 inch bore and a 4

inch stroke. And the whole thing weighs just 152 pounds.

The Wrights figured out they need 8 or 9 horsepower to get off the ground. When we tested the thing, she gave us 16 horsepower for a few seconds, and then she dropped down to a steady 12. It works out to 1,200 rpm, which ~~ain't~~ isn't too shabby and more'n they expected.

We screwed the engine onto the lower wing just to the right of where the pilot will lay. The fuel tank is long and thin and holds a quart and a half of gasoline. That's enough for 18 minutes. We attatched it to a strut near the upper wing. There's no fuel pump. The fuel drips into the engine by gravity. We'll spark the engine with a dry battery and then take it away so to save on weight.

Mr. Wilbur wants to test The Flyer as a glider before we run the engine, but time is running short. They might just go ahead and try to fly her once the propellers are on.

November 5, 1903

I figured they could just take a propeller off a boat and put it on an aeroplane, but nothing doing. If the boat's propeller is just a little too short or the angle is off, the boat still moves in the water. But on a aeroplane the thing ~~don't~~ doesn't get off the ground. Mr. Wilbur and Mr. Orville had to make their OWN durn propellers, just like they made their own durn engine and just like they made their own durn aeroplane.

Mr. Orville explained to me that a propeller works just like a wing that is spinning round in circles. The air pressure is higher behind the blade than it is in the front, so it moves forward. And how fast it moves depends on how fast the propeller is spinning and what angle the blade hits the air. The propeller ~~don't~~ doesn't provide ~~no~~ any lift at all, just forward thrust.

It's powerful complicated cause nothing stays in one durn place. The flying machine is movin' forward, the air is movin' backward, and the propeller is turning sideways. I'll say one thing, after Mr. Orville told me all this, my HEAD was spinning like a propeller.

But he and his brother figured it all out with arithmetic. They calculated that two props spinning slow make more thrust than one prop spinning fast. They calculated they needed 305 revolutions to get 100 pound of thrust. They calculated out everything and tested it in their wind tunnel back in Ohio, so they know it works. They are pretty durn smart for two boys who never even graduated high school.

I done my share of whittling, and these props are cut good. They're 8 foot long and made of spruce, with three layers of wood glued together. The tips are covered with canvas and coated with aluminum paint so they won't split.

We mounted the props on shafts 10 feet apart, and they're driven by chains running over sprockets, just like on a bicycle. That figures, cause Mr. Wilbur and Mr. Orville make bicycles back home. The props are behind the wings so as to not stir up the air as it hits the front of the wings.

Mr. Wilbur says the two propellers are gonna turn in opposite directions, and I ask why.

"If they both turned in the same direction, the force would spin the aeroplane around in circles. By spinning in opposite directions, they will cancel each other out."

I tell you, these Wright boys think of everything.

Isn't it wonderful that all these secrets have been preserved for so many years just so that we could discover them?

—Orville Wright, June 7, 1903

November 6, 1903

The Flyer is done and finished! It's just as well cause the new supply of grub ain't hasn't come in yet, and the Wrights are down to eating powdered milk and crackers. I got 'em some fish, and they appreciated it.

But they got worse problems. Turns out The Flyer weighs 70 pound more'n they figured it would, and they're gonna need 10 more pound of thrust. Mr. Orville reckons they got enough to get off the ground, but just barely. Mr. Wilbur ain't isn't so sure.

When we started up the engine to test the propellers, it was a big mess. The engine jerked and backfired and run so rough that the propeller shafts broke right off! Mr. Wilbur does get disencouraged sometimes, but I never seen him so gloomy. He looked like he had it with the whole thing. He could of fixed the props, but he ain't got the tools here.

Mr. Orville says he ~~ain't~~ isn't giving up. He's gonna take the props back to Ohio and fix 'em in the bike shop. Doc Spratt says let HIM go instead cause he can't take the durn cold air here anyhow. So Doc Spratt goes off to Kitty Hawk with the props to catch the next boat out.

In the middle of all this who shows up but that old gasbag Octave Chanute!

I tell Mr. Wilbur that Chanute is nothing but trouble and we ~~ain't~~ haven't got enough grub to feed him anyway, but Mr. Wilbur hushes me and pretends he is happy to see the old coot. As least he didn't bring that thieving spy Herring with him this time.

Chanute looks over The Flyer and says nobody never tried to fly ~~no~~ a 700 pound machine before. I say there's always a first time for everything, and he looks at me like I'm a bug.

They pulled out last year's glider, ~~drug~~ dragged it up to Big Hill, and put on a nice show for the old coot, but I knew Mr. Wilbur and Mr. Orville were tore up about the busted props. They want to fly for real.

November 11, 1903

You can't fly if you ~~ain't got~~ don't have propellers, so I stayed away from the Wright camp for a couple days. When I went back, Mr. Wilbur looks all sore. Turns out that in the spring that old coot Chanute gave a lecture in France, and he told all about the

Wright glider to a heap of flying machine inventors. He even showed 'em PICTURES of it! Now every crackpot in Paris is building their own aeroplane.

When I show up, Mr. Wilbur is waving a magazine article in Chanute's face that tells all about the lecture in France.

"What did I do?" Chanute keeps saying, all innocent.

"We were not prepared to reveal this information at this time!" says Mr. Wilbur.

Chanute says scientists should share everything they learn for the good of humanity, and Mr. Wilbur says he ~~don't~~ doesn't want ~~nobody~~ anybody stealing his secrets and getting credit for 'em after he and Mr. Orville worked so hard to discover 'em.

Mr. Wilbur was nearbout as sore as I ever seen him. Mr. Orville calmed him down some, but nobody was talking to anybody else, and I didn't want to stick round to hear 'em say nothin'.

November 12, 1903

That old coot Chanute went home. He said he had business to tend to, but I reckon he didn't like the cold, he didn't like eating crackers for dinner, and he didn't like Mr. Wilbur being sore at him. We took him to Kitty Hawk, where we saw a newspaper article that says Langley is gonna make another try any day.

No sign of the propellers. The Wrights don't like setting round doing nothing. Mr. Wilbur spends hours checking his calculations and tinkering with the engine to make it run smooth. Mr. Orville is learning hisself German and French out of a book he has.

It was too dull for me, so I went home. Chloe Beasley spots

me and says where were you, playing with your crazy dingbatter friends? I told her any day those crazy dingbatters are gonna fly their aeroplane and prove they ~~ain't~~ aren't crazy. She just laughed. I told her she needs a good thrashing where she sits down.

November 19, 1903

The Wrights got nothing left to eat 'cept crackers and rice cakes. A package arrived at Kitty Hawk, but it weren't grub and it weren't propellers. It was a pair of gloves, sent as a present from that old coot Chanute. He must feel bad that he made Mr. Wilbur sore.

November 20, 1903

The durn propellers finally arrived, and some grub, too. We put the props on, but they wouldn't tighten. Mr. Orville got a can of Arnstein's hard cement, this goop they use on bicycle rims. He says it can fix anything from a stopwatch to a threshing machine. We heated the shafts and sprockets and poured Arnstein's into the threads. Then we screwed 'em together.

It worked. We tested the engine and drive chains, and they run good, even though they make enough racket to turn a feller deaf.

Around suppertime some surfmen from the Kitty Hawk Life Saving Station come by with extra fish they couldn't eat. The Wrights tell 'em they are gonna test The Flyer in a couple of days, and they will need helpers to tote the thing. Mr. Wilbur said he would tack a bedsheet up on the side of the shed as a signal for 'em to come on over.

November 26, 1903

Today is Thanksgiving. They ~~was~~ were all ready to take out The Flyer when some weather set in. It begun to rain, and even snow a bit. The Wrights didn't sit around doing nothing while they were waiting. They rigged up a stopwatch, counter, and anemometer to The Flyer so if she DOES fly, they'll know how long, how far, and how many times the props turn.

We did some indoor tests with the engine and props too. At first they were turning at only 306 rpm, but Mr. Wilbur tinkered with the engine and got her up to 333 and then 359. That made 'em happy.

They didn't have no turkey for Thanksgiving, but Mr. Orville went out and shot a chicken and we ate it.

November 28, 1903

Saturday. The weather was unfitting for flying. Howling winds and snow flurries. It is getting too cold to work outside for more than a few minutes at a time, even with Chanute's gloves on. The water in the washbasin was froze up this morning.

I was in the shed with Mr. Wilbur and he was looking over the props when he suddenly stops and sits down on a chair. Then he puts his head in his hands.

"What's wrong?" I say.

He don't say nothing at first, and then he says real slow, "There is a crack in one of the propeller shafts."

He doesn't cuss or nothing, of course. He just sits there like a dead man. I go get Mr. Orville, and he looks at the crack. Then he sits on the chair next to his brother and puts his arm around him. He tells Mr. Wilbur how lucky they are that they spied the crack when The Flyer was on the ground. If they tried to fly the thing with a propeller on the bum, one of 'em probably would of died.

That didn't cheer up Mr. Wilbur much. But nothing really cheers Mr. Wilbur up when he's down, and nothing gets Mr. Orville down when he's up, which is usually.

After a while Mr. Orville just stands up, goes over to the bum prop, and starts to unscrew it. Mr. Wilbur finally looks up and sees what his brother is doin'. Then after a few minutes HE gets up without saying anything. He goes over to the other prop and unscrews that one.

We took Mr. Orville over to the Kitty Hawk wharf to catch the next boat out. He's going back to Ohio hisself to make a new set of propellers.

December 1, 1903

Don't it just figure that as soon as Mr. Orville was gone, it warms up and the weather is perfect for flying? I stopped over to the Wright camp to check up on Mr. Wilbur. He was mostly writing letters, fetching wood for the stove, and splitting it. He looks lonely and sad.

Mr. Wilbur says he saw a newspaper at Kitty Hawk, and it said Langley will be ready for another test any day. I just hope Mr. Orville gets back with the new propellers quick.

December 11, 1903

Friday. It's two weeks till Christmas now, and I was starting to think Mr. Orville was just gonna stay home for good and forget about the durn propellers. But then he comes running into camp pushing a cart with the two props and waving a newspaper over his head like a crazy man.

"Did you hear?" he hollers. "Did you hear the news?"

I didn't hear nothing, so he shows me and Mr. Wilbur the newspaper.

Turns out Langley's flying machine flipped upside down and dropped into the river like a shovelful of mud. I let out a whoop and a holler.

"Langley is finished!" I yell. "Finished!"

AIRSHIP BREAKS IN TWO.

Prof. Langley's Second Attempt to Fly Fails Completely — Prof. Manly Drops Into Icy Potomac.

WASHINGTON, Dec. 8.—Under weather conditions which were regarded as perfect, the Langley airship, or aeroplane, was given a second trial to-day a short distance from Washington down the Potomac. The result was the complete wreck of the airship.

Everything had been in readiness for the trial for some days, and it was felt that all that was necessary for a successful test was the right sort of wind and weather. This afternoon these conditions presented themselves.

On the signal to start, the aeroplane glided smoothly along the launching tramway until the end of the slide was reached. Then, left to itself, the aeroplane broke in two and turned completely over, precipitating Prof. Charles Manly, who was operating it, into icy water beneath the tangled mass.

"I don't ordinarily rejoice at the misfortunes of others," says Mr. Orville, "but in this case, I'll make an exception."

I thought I might could even see a little smile creep into Mr. Wilbur's face for the first time in I don't know how long.

"Professor Langley has had his fling," he said. "It seems to be our turn to throw now."

We hope that Prof. Langley will not put his substantial greatness as a scientist in further peril by continuing to waste his time, and the money involved, in further airship experiments. Life is short, and he is capable of services to humanity incomparably greater than can be expected to result from trying to fly.

—the *New York Times*, December 10, 1903

In the past we have paid our respects to the humorous aspects of the Langley flying machine, its repeated and disastrous failures, the absurd atmosphere of secrecy in which it was enveloped, and the imposing and expensive pageantry that attended its various manifestations. It now seems to us, however, that the time is ripe for a really serious appraisement of the so-called aeroplane and for a withdrawal by the government from all further participation in its financial and scientific calamities.

—the *Washington Post*, December 1903

December 12, 1903

We installed the new props and brought The Flyer outside for the first time. I was excited cause after all they been through, they were finally fixing to fly the thing.

Only problem was the wind didn't breeze up. We kept waiting around and it never did. With nothing better to do, we slid The Flyer up and down the track just to make dead sure it worked.

Time is getting short. Christmas is 13 days away, and I know Mr. Wilbur and Mr. Orville will be going home for the holiday whether they fly or not. It will take 'em a few days to get back to Ohio, so I reckon if they don't get The Flyer in the air this week, they never will.

December 13, 1903

Sunday. You'd think with just 12 days left they might break the durn Sabbath and fly. But nothing doin'. The wind was just right, too. No use hanging round, so I went a-fishin'.

December 14, 1903

The weather was perfect, so I rode over to the Wright camp quick as a scared rabbit. When I get there, Mr. Wilbur was tacking a bedsheet up to the side of the shed. He says he wants some surfmen at the Kitty Hawk Life Saving Station to come on over and be witnesses in case The Flyer gets off the ground.

"I'll be your witness," I say.

He didn't say it in a mean way, but he says, "Johnny, you told us you stuffed a dead calf with straw to fool its mother. People may not believe you if you tell them you saw a flying machine."

"It was the TRUTH about the calf!" I say, but he said he was putting up the bedsheet just the same.

Soon a few surfmen show up, along with two boys and a dog who happened by. There weren't enough wind to take off from the level sand, so we had to bring The Flyer out to the bottom of Big Hill. She was too heavy to tote, so we rolled her on the Grand Junction Railroad, picking up one section from the back of The Flyer and putting it in the front as she rolled along. It took nearbout 40 minute.

Finally we get her out there and everything looks set. The wind was 5 mile per hour. Mr. Wilbur and Mr. Orville flip a coin, and Mr. Wilbur wins. He gets the first chance to fly.

They start up the engine, and The Flyer is clattering and popping and snorting and shaking like a wild horse. The boys and the dog dash away all scared. The props was are spinning awful fast. Mr. Wilbur clum aboard and lay there for a minute or more while the engine warmed up. Mr. Orville went to hold the right wingtip, and I took the left.

"If she flies," I shout over the racket, "I'll run to Kitty Hawk and tell everybody the news."

"I may just FLY over there and tell them MYSELF," Mr. Wilbur says.

He looked to both sides and nodded his head. Then he opened the clip to release the rope that was holding the aeroplane in place. She starts sliding down the rail, slow at first, then fast. Me and Mr. Orville run with her to steady her, but soon we couldn't keep up with her, and she lifts off the rail.

SHE'S FLYIN'!

She rose up sharp maybe 15 foot high, and then she just stops there, like maybe she changed her mind or something. Then she falls back and clanks down on the left wing, swinging the aeroplane around.

We all run over. Mr. Wilbur is okay, but one of the elevator supports was splintered and a skid was busted. Mr. Wilbur cut the engine. The stopwatch said 3.5 seconds.

"It was my fault," Mr. Wilbur says. "I pointed it up too fast. I was overanxious."

"Still, she flew," I say. "You got her off the ground."

"It wasn't a real flight," Mr. Wilbur says. "It doesn't count."

December 15, 1903

Spent all day Tuesday repairing The Flyer. Ten days till Christmas.

December 16, 1903

Repairs done by noon. We moved the rails to level ground so The Flyer wouldn't pick up so much speed so fast on takeoff. They ~~was~~ were ready to try again, but the wind died kind of sudden.

The wind breezed up again, but then we see a line of black clouds gathering down the beach apiece. The surf was rumbling, and we got The Flyer into the hangar just before the rains come.

Don't look like there will be any flying tomorrow, and it's only nine days left till Christmas. The Wrights got to light out for Ohio in a few days. Don't look like it'll be a Merry Christmas for them this year.

December 17, 1903

Thursday. It looked like a dirty day. The rain stopped, but it was gray and so cold that puddles of water froze up. I figured they wouldn't fly, but I rode over to the Wright camp for the heck of it.

When I get there, Mr. Wilbur is a-shaving and Mr. Orville is fussing with the stove. They had on their usual white collar shirts and jackets and ties, like they ~~was~~ were going to a fancy dinner party or something.

They were havin' a discussion about whether or not they should fly. The weather weren't exactly fitting. Mr. Wilbur says the wind is blowing 22-27 miles per hour from the north, and it will be dangerous. Mr. Orville says they could wait some, but he was itching to fly and then go home for Christmas. I told 'em the longer they hang around, the colder it is gonna get.

They decided to try, and Mr. Orville tacked up the bedsheet. While we ~~was~~ were waiting for the witnesses to show up, we pinned the launch rail to the sand about 200 foot west of the shed. We faced it into the wind south to north on level ground. It was powerful cold, and we had to go inside to warm up at the stove every few minutes.

Soon some of the surfmen from Kitty Hawk show. I recognized Big John Daniels cause he's just about the biggest man I ever seen. He come with Will Dough, a fisherman and farmer I'd seen around, and a lumberman named Ceef Brinkley. There was this feller named Adam Etheridge, too. We all grabbed The Flyer and toted her out to the rail. She weighed more'n 600 pound, and it weren't easy. We rested her right wing on a wood bench to hold her steady.

Mr. Orville brought out the big camera and set it on one of them tripod thingamajigs to the right of The Flyer. He slipped a glass plate into it. Then he aimed it at the end of the rail and told Big John to snap a photograph if The Flyer raised up at all.

"But I ain't never took a photograph in my life," Big John says.

"It's just like shootin' a rifle," Mr. Orville says. He showed him how to duck his head under the black cloth and told him to squeeze this rubber bulb when the time was right.

It was ten thirty, and they were ready for a try. Mr. Wilbur and Mr. Orville walked off to the side and stood close together. I couldn't hear 'em cause they was talking low. Then they shook hands and held on for a few seconds too long, like one of 'em was going away on a trip and wouldn't be back for a long time.

They walked around The Flyer for one more check. Mr. Wilbur pumped a few drops of gas into each cylinder. He sparked the engine, and then his brother and he each grabbed a propeller and gave a pull. The engine coughed awake, and the props commenced to turn.

It was Mr. Orville's turn cause Mr. Wilbur had his try on Monday. Mr. Orville shed his bowler hat and put on a cap. Then he clum into The Flyer and lay down belly buster style next to the engine. He worked the elevator up and down and moved his hips back and forth to check the rudder and wing warping. Then he nodded to Mr. Wilbur, who was at the right wingtip.

Just then, this bird flies by. A hawk, I reckon. She swoops down like she's taking a good look at The Flyer, and then she flies away. We all look up at it. I see Mr. Wilbur and Mr. Orville looking at each other with little smiles on their faces. I know what they must of been thinking. If The Flyer flies, birds are gonna need to share the sky for the first time ever.

Mr. Etheridge was holding the anemometer, and he said the wind was at 27 mile per hour. The rest of us stood there all quiet and shivering in the cold.

"Don't look sad," Mr. Wilbur hollers over the engine noise. "Laugh, holler, clap."

We did as he said, and Mr. Wilbur pulled out the bench from under the wing. He nodded back to Mr. Orville.

Mr. Orville released the rope that was holding The Flyer back, and she begun to roll down the rail, slow. Much slower than on Monday. Mr. Wilbur walked with her, holding the wingtip. Then he had to run to keep up.

Nearbout 40 feet down the rail The Flyer heisted up! Gosh blame it, SHE HEISTS UP! It was like magic.

She rose slow, nice and gentle, to 5 foot up or so. We all start in with whoops and hollers. After a few seconds she darts for the ground, but Mr. Orville must have worked the elevator, cause she darts up again just before she would of hit sand.

She darts down again and then up again. Mr. Orville was trying to hold her steady, but she keeps dinking up and down like a monkey. Finally she skids to a hard stop nearbout 120 foot away, and we all run over with more whoops and hollers.

The first flight lasted only twelve seconds, a flight very modest compared with that of birds, but it was, nevertheless, the first in the history of the world in which a machine carrying a man had raised itself by its own power into the air in free flight, had sailed forward on a level course without reduction of speed, and had finally landed without being wrecked.

—**Orville and Wilbur Wright**

When we get to Mr. Orville, tears was streaming down his face. Mr. Wilbur grabs him like a long lost buddy. They look at the stopwatch but is says zero cause it must of reset itself when The Flyer hit the ground. Mr. Orville reckons it was around 12 seconds in the air.

"Not long enough," says Mr. Wilbur. "We had glides that lasted a minute. We have to do better."

12 seconds was good enough for ME. I hopped on my bicycle and rode down the beach to Kitty Hawk.

"THEY DONE IT! THEY DONE IT!" I hollered to anybody I saw. "DAMN'D IF THEY AIN'T FLEW!" I felt like I was Paul Revere or something, saying the British were a-comin'.

By the time I get back to camp, they are getting ready for another try after fixing one of the skids that broke. Mr. Wilbur clum on this time. We launched The Flyer, and he flew her 175 foot in 15 seconds. It was all up and down like the first time. We whooped and hollered again, and then toted her back to the rail for another go.

Mr. Orville took his turn this time. He was going good, and a nice blow of wind heists The Flyer up near 15 foot and tilts her. Mr. Orville was able to right her and one wing touched the sand first when he landed. It was 200 foot this time.

It was near noon by then, and Mr. Wilbur clum on for one more ride before lunch. The Flyer started out all up and down like before, but after a couple hunnerd foot she smoothes out, and then she's going straight as an arrow, nice and gentle, like she was still on rails or something! She's soaring like a bird, and she looks like she ain't never isn't ever gonna come down. We all run down the beach chasing her, but we didn't catch her.

Mr. Wilbur stayed up there for a whole 59 seconds. That's one second short of a MINUTE! When he finally lands we measure it off and it come to 852 foot from the start point! Even Mr. Wilbur was satisfied with that.

It weren't much fun toting The Flyer back, but we were all so excited it was tolerable. We were almost to the rail when Mr. Orville leans over to me and whispers, "Johnny, do you know how you are always pestering me for a ride and I always say not today?" I say yeah, and he says, "I think today might be the day."

Well, I would of jumped right out of my shoes if I had shoes to jump out of. Finally I was gonna get my chance!

We set The Flyer down a few feet west of the shed. They had to fix the right skid, which busted a little on the last landing. Mr. Wilbur and Mr. Orville was jawing about how to fix it when this boisterous gust come out of nowhere. It gets up under the left wingtip and picks her up.

"Grab it!" Mr. Orville shouts, but it weren't no use cause the wind picked the whole Flyer up sideways. Mr. Wilbur took hold of the front. Big John Daniels jumped onto the thing, but even Big John couldn't hold her down. The Flyer rolled over and the wind kept a-comin' and soon she was cartwheelin' toward the beach with Big John holding on for his life.

The engine broke loose, and I could hear the wires snapping and wood cracking and Big John crying out. It was a horrible sound. It looked like The Flyer might be blown right into the ocean with Big John inside.

But then the wind stops just like it started. Big John was tangled up in the wires and chains, but he staggers out with no broken bones, but just some cuts and bruises. The Flyer was in worse shape. All the wing ribs was broken and so was the crankcase. It was a mess of junk.

We dragged the wreck back to the hangar. Mr. Wilbur and Mr. Orville weren't too sad cause, after all, they DID fly the thing—four times, no less. They did what they set out to do four years ago, something nobody never done in the history of the world.

The only sad one was me cause I was counting on getting that ride.

"I'm sorry, Johnny," Mr. Orville says as we toted the junk back. I knew there was no point in fixing The Flyer. It was getting too cold anyhow, and the Wrights had to be heading home to Ohio.

The surfmen went back to the lifesaving station. The Wrights had lunch and said they ~~was~~ were gonna go over to Kitty Hawk to send a telegram. I went home happy and sad both at the same time.

Form No. 168.

THE WESTERN UNION TELEGRAPH COMPANY.
INCORPORATED
23,000 OFFICES IN AMERICA. CABLE SERVICE TO ALL THE WORLD.

This Company TRANSMITS and DELIVERS messages only on conditions limiting its liability, which have been assented to by the sender of the following message.
Errors can be guarded against only by repeating a message back to the sending station for comparison, and the Company will not hold itself liable for errors or delay
in transmission or delivery of Unrepeated Messages, beyond the amount of tolls paid thereon, nor in any case where the claim is not presented in writing within sixty days
after the message is filed with the Company for transmission.
This is an UNREPEATED MESSAGE, and is delivered by request of the sender, under the conditions named above.
ROBERT C. CLOWRY, President and General Manager.

170

RECEIVED at

176 C KA CS 33 Paid.   Via Norfolk Va

Kitty Hawk N C Dec 17

Bishop M Wright

7 Hawthorne St

Success four flights thursday morning all against twenty one mile

wind started from Level with engine power alone average speed

through air thirty one miles longest 57 seconds inform Press

home Christmas .

Orevelle Wright   525P.

Book 5: 1908
RETURN TO KILL DEVIL HILL

The Wrights have flown or they have not flown.
They possess a machine or they do not possess
one. They are in fact fliers or liars.

—*New York Herald*, **February 1906**

January 1, 1908

What's it been, 4 years or more since I stopped keeping a diary? So much has happened. There was that horrible earthquake in San Francisco that killed around 700 people. Oklahoma became the 46th state. Teddy Roosevelt was reelected President. And I became old enough to vote!

They say they're broadcasting radio now, but I haven't heard it. Ford is coming out with this new car called the Model T. It used to be only rich folks could buy an automobile. But this one is only going to cost $850, so I hope to own one someday.

Mama said now that I am all grown up, it is time to be on my own. So I got my own place in Nags Head, and I am a real businessman now! I started a company taking dingbatters hunting and fishing. I have to pay bills and keep the books and so forth. I'm not getting rich or anything, but it sure beats getting a real job.

Since their successful flights in December of 1903, I haven't heard a thing about the Wright brothers. I wonder what happened to them. The wind and rain and sand are starting to rip the old Wright camp apart.

The only thing I saw in the newspaper about flying machines

was that Samuel Langley died in 1906. I haven't seen any aeroplanes flying around. What the Wright brothers accomplished didn't change the world or anything like I expected.

It's almost like what I saw that day at Kill Devil Hill never happened. When I used to tell people I saw a real flying machine in 1903, they'd look at me like I was crazy. I never could convince Chloe Beasley of what I saw.

After a while I just stopped telling people about the flying machine. I stopped going over to Kill Devil Hill looking for the Wright brothers. They didn't come back in 1904 or 1905 or 1906 or 1907. I began to wonder if I had really witnessed a flying machine at all.

March 6, 1908

Happy birthday to ME! I am 23. Mama says it is time I think about settling down and starting a family. I say, "Where am I going to find a gal around HERE to marry?" She says, "What about Chloe Beasley? I know you've had your eye on her." I tell Mama, "I do NOT have my eye on Chloe," even though I sure do.

That little squirt has turned into a real dasher. I saw her the other day over at the general store where she works, and she doesn't look like a little girl anymore. She got curves now, and she is turning out prettier than a sunset.

I went up to Chloe at the store and said, "How would you like to be my sweetheart?" She said, "Johnny Moore, you are ten whole years older than me, and I don't know if I can be the sweetheart of a man that old."

I reminded Chloe that she was catching up to me, and while ten years seemed like a long time NOW, someday when I was 60 and she was 50, we would just be two old folks sitting on rocking chairs together. She told me that herself.

She threw me a little smile, but she didn't say she would be my sweetheart, and she didn't say she wouldn't be my sweetheart. All she said was, "We'll see about that."

Now I know Chloe MUST be a grown up woman, because if she was still a girl, she would have just answered with a simple yes or no instead of leaving me wondering what the heck she meant.

May 13, 1908

Guess what? The Cubs are in first place! Never thought I would hear myself saying THAT. So far they won 13 games and lost 6. It's still early, so anything can happen. But it looks like they have a great team this year. Nobody pulls off the double play like Tinker to Evers to Chance.

I bumped into my old chum Elijah Baum today, and he says did I hear the news? I say no I did not, and after forcing me to guess what the news was for half an hour, Elijah finally tells me "those crazy" Wright brothers are back in town.

Now I know Elijah has always been a big fat liar and always WILL BE a big fat liar. So I don't believe anything he says. But he says, "Go over to Kitty Hawk and see for yourself if you don't believe me." So I did.

Well, old Elijah was speaking the honest truth for once in his life, because when I got to the Kitty Hawk Life Saving Station, who did I see having a cup of coffee with the surfmen but Mr. Wilbur and Mr. Orville Wright.

They were powerful happy to see me, and me them. I am

much taller than the Wright Brothers now, and Mr. Orville asked me, "How's the weather up there?" and other jokes like that. They thought it was real funny that I have taken to wearing shoes and dressing more respectable.

I asked where have they been all these years, and they said they haven't flown since 1905. They had been hoping to sell their aeroplane to the United States government, but after Professor Langley dumped his flying machine (and $70,000) into the river, the government wasn't interested in flying machines anymore. The government must have figured that if the famous scientist Samuel Langley couldn't fly, a couple of bicycle mechanics from Ohio sure couldn't either.

I said, "Why didn't you just fly your aeroplane over The White House or something? THAT would show 'em." But Mr. Wilbur said they were afraid to let anybody see them fly because there were spies like Herring everywhere looking to steal their invention.

> We had hoped in 1906 to sell our invention to governments for enough money to satisfy our needs and then devote our time to science, but the jealousy of certain persons blocked this plan. . . . It is always easier to deal with things than with men, and no one can direct his life entirely as he would choose.

—**Wilbur Wright, January 1912**

So I asked them why they came back to the Outer Banks NOW. They said they finally got their patent on their flying machine, and the U.S. government and the government of France were finally interested in buying aeroplanes. They had to prove their aeroplane was perfected, so they'd come back to Kitty Hawk to test a new machine. Mr. Wilbur invited me to come by their camp tomorrow to see it.

May 14, 1908

The new aeroplane is a beauty. They call it the Wright Type A Flyer. The pilot doesn't lay on his stomach anymore. Now he sits up in a little seat. There's a seat for a passenger on the right of the pilot too. Both seats have their own set of controls.

The new Flyer weighs around 800 pounds, and it looks more sturdy than the one I remember from 1903. Mr. Orville told me they have already flown it back in Ohio for 5 minutes or more without coming down. They can even fly in circles and figure 8s.

I had my eye on that passenger seat. I didn't want to ask for a ride the way I did all the time when I was a boy, because sometimes the Wrights got angry. I have acquired some degree of politeness over the years. But I figured it would be okay to hint.

"Do you and Mr. Orville go up in this thing together?" I asked Mr. Wilbur.

"Oh, no," he said. "We made a promise to each other long ago that we would never do that. If we were in the same aeroplane and we were killed in a crash, there would be nobody left to continue our work."

That made sense to me. I was walking around the machine

trying to figure out a way to ask who sat in the passenger seat, when Mr. Orville piped up.

"We DO need to test The Flyer with a passenger, Johnny," he says. "Do you want a ride?"

"You MEAN it?"

"Sure I mean it. Let's go."

Well, I climbed through the rods and wires into that passenger seat faster than a trout stealing bait. I put my feet up on a bar in front of me. The Wrights gave the propellers a pull, and the engine started clattering and chattering. I suppose I should have been a little scared, but I was too excited to be scared.

Mr. Orville climbed into the pilot seat beside me. There was a string hanging down in front of me, and Mr. Orville told me not to touch it because it stops the engine automatically. That way, if there's a crash, the passenger is thrown forward and hits the string to cut the engine.

I buttoned my coat. Mr. Orville told me to pull my cap down so it wouldn't blow off. I heard the propellers behind me.

"Are you afraid of heights?" he asked me, and I said I didn't know because I'd never been in anything that was very high.

He laughed and reached down to release the anchoring wire. The aeroplane lurched forward on the rail like a horse bolting. It kept picking up speed, and when half the rail was gone, Mr. Orville pulled back on the controls.

I felt something happening, like I was getting lightheaded. I looked down and saw the ground shooting by me backwards and all blurry. And then the earth dropped away and I felt like my stomach had fallen off.

I wasn't convinced that we were flying at first. It felt like there had to be an invisible track underneath the aeroplane, holding it up. But there wasn't, of course. My hat flew off, and I didn't care one bit.

"I'M FLYING!" I hollered, and I let out a whoop they probably heard over in Cape Hatteras. Mr. Orville laughed. The wind was whipping through my hair. A bird was flying around, and I yelled, "GET OUT OF OUR WAY, BIRD!"

We climbed above the trees, and I got a sudden feeling in my ears like my head was about to explode. Mr. Orville saw the look on my face.

"IT'S THE AIR PRESSURE!" he shouts, though I could barely hear him over the engine. "IT'S PERFECTLY NORMAL. SWALLOW!"

I did and I felt a little pop in my ears and I felt better.

Everything looked so small down on the ground, like little toys. I could see way out into the ocean on one side and Albemarle Sound on the other. It didn't feel like we were moving fast anymore. It didn't feel like we were moving at ALL.

I could see the trees and houses going by slowly. We were heading down the beach in the direction of Nags Head. Off in the distance I could see the Beasleys' house, but I couldn't see mine or mama's yet.

A wind came along and bumped us up some. Mr. Orville yelled for me to hold on. He moved the control and the right wing went up and we were tilted, and I felt like I was going to fall out. Then I realized he was just banking into a turn.

"SEE?" he yelled real loud in my ear. "IT'S LIKE RIDING A BICYCLE!"

He was about to turn back up the beach when I saw somebody way down below hanging wash on a clothesline. I peered at her and I realized it was Chloe Beasley.

"HEY, CHLOE!" I shouted. "LOOK AT ME!"

She was looking up at the aeroplane, but we were too high for her to see me or hear me.

"IS THAT YOUR GAL?" Mr. Orville shouted in my ear.

"YES," I shouted back. He brought the plane down some for a better look.

"SHE'S PRETTY," he says. "YOU LOVE HER?"

"I RECKON SO!"

"ARE YOU GOING TO MARRY HER?"

"IF SHE'LL HAVE ME."

Mr. Orville brought the aeroplane down lower, and we were doing lazy circles over Chloe. Now I could see her good. She was just looking up at us with her mouth open like she'd seen a ghost or something.

"HEY, CHLOE!" I yelled, waving at her. "IT'S ME, JOHNNY MOORE! DO YOU BELIEVE IN FLYING MACHINES NOW?"

Chloe looked like she couldn't talk, and even if she could I wouldn't have been able to hear what she was saying. She still had her mouth open and she started waving at me.

"WHY DON'T YOU ASK HER?" Mr. Orville yelled in my ear.

"ASK HER WHAT?"

"ASK HER TO MARRY YOU."

"RIGHT NOW?"

"WHY NOT?"

He circled back toward Chloe and brought us down as low as he could. She was still craning her neck, waving and laughing.

"HEY CHLOE!" I shouted down at her. "HOW ABOUT YOU AND ME GETTING MARRIED?"

I don't know if she heard me or not. She yelled some word back. It could have been "YES" and it could have been "NO," but I'm pretty sure it was, "WHAT?"

Mr. Orville said we ought to be getting back because he didn't want to run out of fuel. I waved to Chloe again, and Mr. Orville turned us back up the beach.

"WAS IT FUN?" Mr. Orville yelled to me when we were about a mile from Kill Devil Hill. I told him yes, and he said if I liked THAT, I'm really going to like THIS. And the next thing I knew, the engine noise stopped. I turned around. The propellers weren't turning anymore.

"WE'RE GOING TO CRASH!" I screamed, grabbing my seat.

But we didn't. Mr. Orville just laughed, and we went into a slow glide the rest of the way. Without the engine and propellers going, it was quiet like the middle of the night. When we touched down, I barely felt the skids hit the sand.

October 14, 1908

I don't believe in impossible things anymore, because two impossible things happened today.

The first impossible thing was THE CHICAGO CUBS BEAT THE DETROIT TIGERS TO WIN THE WORLD SERIES! Don't that beat all? The Cubs are the world champs!

The second impossible thing was that CHLOE BEASLEY AND I FINALLY SET THE DATE! We are going to be hitched on August 9, 1910. I wanted to get married sooner, but Chloe's mama won't let her until she turns 15, so I guess that's all right with me.

Shucks, the way I look at it, if the Cubs can win the World Series, and if a regular feller like me can marry a pretty gal like Chloe Beasley, and if people can go flying around in machines . . . well, I reckon just about ANYTHING is possible.

In Conclusion:
FACTS AND FICTIONS

What Happened to Johnny and Chloe?

Johnny Moore and Chloe Beasley got married in 1910, when he was twenty-five and she was fifteen (this was not so unusual in those days). They had fourteen children and named one of them Orville.

I tried to show Johnny's personality accurately, but for the sake of this story I exaggerated his involvement with the Wright brothers. Johnny *did* witness the first flight on December 17, 1903, and he probably had been an observer at the Wright camp before that day, but he was not a daily presence, and he never got a ride in the flyer. In fact, Johnny Moore never rode in an airplane in his entire life.

The stories about Johnny going around barefoot and stuffing the dead calf to fool its mother are true. Johnny did love to fish and grew up to become a fishing and hunting guide. He lived near Kitty Hawk all his life. Every so often people would knock on his front door and ask him if he was the same Johnny Moore who witnessed the first flight. His response was usually, "Yup, that's me. Wanna go fishing?"

Johnny Moore was the last surviving witness to the first flight. He died on February 28, 1952, at the age of sixty-six. Chloe (who never did learn to read) died on January 15, 1963. She was sixty-seven.

So she *did* finally catch up with Johnny.

Last Witness to First Flight Takes Washington With Shrug

(handwritten) Mercury 1948 After

Johnny Moore, Who at 15 Helped the Wright Brothers, Uses Barlow Knife to Cut Meat in Swank Hotel

Washington, Dec. 19.—Johnny Moore, the man of the hour when the Kitty Hawk, the Wright Brothers' famed first successful airplane, was formally unveiled in its new resting place in the Smithsonian Institution, has gone back to North Carolina's Outer Banks apparently totally unimpressed by the splendor of Washington or by the attention paid him.

Moore, who showed he puts convenience and efficiency ahead of convention by whipping out a Barlow knife to cut some tough spareribs served at dinner in the swank Hotel Lafayette here, is the lone survivor of the small group who aided or witnessed the first flight of the Kitty Hawk near his home in 1903.

And, as such, he was probably the most sought-out of all the people who attended the Kitty Hawk unveiling Friday—scores of famed aviation figures shook hands with him, and he was by all odds the most interviewed and photographed figure present.

More Interested in Fishing

But, while Moore amiably talked to reporters and others about the first flight, he was obviously more interested in talking about the fishing for which the Outer Banks is famous and about his own activities as a fishing guide.

"I take a lot of parties fishing," he said, "and I make a good living at it. Most I ever made out of this first flight was $17 some writers gave me for telling them the story. But if I had just one dollar for every time I've told it, I'd be richer than that Mr. Rockefeller."

This reporter didn't ask Moore to tell him that familiar story again, but he did get the banksman to admit that he "sure was surprised" when the Kitty Hawk actually flew,

ever will—in fact, he could have flown to Washington, but came instead by automobile. You can't fish from an airplane, in the first place, and Moore just isn't interested.

But with Mrs. Moore, it's different. She never has flown, either—but she certainly would like to and, she indicated, when she recovers her health may do just that.

And Mrs. Moore was more impressed with Washington than was her husband. Moore pointed out that, after all, he had once been to New York—as a member of a dredge crew— but Mrs. Moore confessed that never before had she wandered farther from her banks home than Norfolk, where her two daughters, Mrs. Ella Tillett and Mrs. Marie Dorse, live.

The Moores saw more of the wonders of a scientific world than aircraft while here, Moore, for instance, took part in a coast-to-coast broadcast and, in addition, not only was televised, but had an opportunity to see television in operation. A youthful companion on the trip, diminutive Miss Mary Blanche Meekins, daughter of Victor Meekins, the Moores's host on the trip, was thrilled by television, although she compared it unfavorably with motion pictures. Moore wasn't thrilled a-tall.

"Now," he said, "let me tell you about this party on a fishing trip . . . ."

JOHNNY MOORE NOW SEEN AS A GREAT CELEBRITY
(Elizabeth City Independent)

Johnny Moore of Colington, who has been a celebrity in the minds of Nags Head habitues for a sizeable number of years, has suddenly, because he is the last person who remembers the Wright brothers first flight as an eyewitnesse, become a national celebrity.

Everyone in Elizabeth City who has spent any time at all at Nags Head for the past two generations, knows John Moore and his trosy about not knowing exactly how many kids he has "because oi ain't burned off the marsh yet" which is now being passed by the printed word across the land. It is the only one of the very many quips that Moore has to pass about himself or his family.

Nearly as well known as Johnny Moore is Mrs. Cloe Moore, his wife.

Thirty years ago John lived at Nags Head and made his living in the soft crab trade, but when he got married he moved to Colington, where he settled down o replentishment of the Moore stock in Dare County—a task in which he seemed particularly well adapted since he raised 14 children.

The fact that Johnny is becoming a real celebrity makes all of his Elizabeth City friends, who knew him well, very proud. They figure that it's about time he was getting some national recognition, although all of his friends hope that it does not come with such concentration as to remove the salt from his beard or require him to forget at what stage of the noon the fish will be running at "hoi toid."

To Johnny—our congratulations on the belated recognition.

What happened to Wilbur and Orville?

Shortly after this story ends in 1908, Wilbur sailed for France and Orville went to Washington to publicly demonstrate their flying machine for the first time. Thousands of astonished witnesses in both countries saw the Wright brothers in the air for up to two hours. It had been *five* years since their historic first flight, but the world finally realized it was true—people could fly. The Wright brothers became sudden international celebrities.

You may be wondering, if the Wright brothers invented the airplane, why is there is no Wright Airlines today?

The Wrights were so concerned that competitors were going to steal their invention before they received a patent, they refused to demonstrate their airplane or even let anyone see photos of it. They finally got a patent on May 23, 1906. For the next five years they had to spend nearly all their time suing copycats who infringed on their patent. The Wrights won every lawsuit, but while they were in court, other aviators were building similar planes and improving them.

By 1909 competitors were in the air. Louis Blériot, a Frenchman, flew across the English Channel that year. By 1913 the competition was building better, faster planes than the Wrights. Two years later Orville sold their company (for $1.5 million).

Wilbur Wright made his last flight in 1910. Two years later, on May 30, 1912, Wilbur tragically died of typhoid. He was only forty-five years old.

Orville piloted a plane for the final time on May 13, 1918. He died at the age of seventy-six on January 30, 1948.

I got most of the information for this book by reading other books: *Wilbur and Orville,* by Fred Howard; *The Bishop's Boys* by Tom D. Crouch; *The Wright Brothers,* by Russell Freedman; *First in Flight* by Stephen Kirk; *Triumph at Kitty Hawk* by Thomas Parramore; *How We Invented the Airplane* by Orville Wright; and *Miracle at Kitty Hawk: The Letters of Wilbur and Orville Wright.* Much of the Wright brothers' dialogue is words they actually spoke or wrote in letters and diaries. The dates, locations, and events are accurate.

Yes, Orville really did shoot a mouse.

What Happened to the Other Characters?

Not a single character in this story is fictional. Dan Tate died in 1905, Samuel Langley in 1906, and Octave Chanute in 1910.

Augustus Herring died in 1926, insisting until the end that *he* was the true inventor of the airplane. Doc Spratt died in 1934, and Edward Huffaker in 1937. First flight witnesses Adam Etheridge and W. C. Brinkley both died in 1940. Big John Daniels died in 1948, within twenty-four hours of Orville Wright.

Captain Bill Tate, who first welcomed the Wrights into his home in 1900, outlived all the rest, finally passing away in 1953 at the age of eighty-four. His daughter Irene, who wore a dress made from the Wrights' 1900 glider, grew up to become a pilot herself. She was the first woman to fly round-trip between New York and Miami.

The Good and the Bad

The Wright brothers believed, at least in the beginning, that the invention of the airplane would put an end to all wars. Orville wrote, "We thought governments would realize the impossibility of winning by surprise attacks, and that no country would enter into war with another of equal size when it knew that it would have to win by simply wearing out its enemy."

Obviously, that proved to be wrong. The invention of the airplane opened up a new age of travel and communication. But it also opened up a new age of death and destruction. There is good and bad to every technology.

Good Things

1903: First flight by the Wright brothers
1909: First flight across the English Channel
1910: First flight to take off from water
1918: Regular airmail service begins
1919: First transatlantic flight

1923: First nonstop transcontinental flight

1924: First around-the-world flight

1926: First flight over the North Pole

1927: First solo nonstop flight across the Atlantic

1929: First flight completed entirely with instruments

1931: First flight into the stratosphere

1933: First solo around-the-world flight

1937: First successful helicopter flight

1942: First American jet flight

1947: First flight to break the speed of sound

1949: First nonstop around-the-world flight

1952: Jet airline service begins

1957: First man-made satellite is launched

1961: Yuri Gagarin becomes the first human in space.

1969: Neil Armstrong becomes the first human to walk on the moon. (He brought a piece of the original cloth wing covering from the 1903 Wright flyer with him.)

1977: First successful human-powered flight

1980: First long-distance solar-powered flight

1981: Space shuttle is launched.

1999: First around-the-world balloon flight

2002: Steve Fossett becomes the first person to fly around the world nonstop by balloon.

Bad Things

1908: Thomas Selfridge is the first passenger killed in an airplane crash. The pilot is Orville Wright, who is severely injured.

1910: Ralph Johnstone is the first American pilot to die in a plane crash. Within two years a hundred pilots would be killed.

1914: First aerial combat as World War I begins

1915: First air raids on England

1918: World War I ends, with 55,000 people killed in aerial combat. Orville Wright wrote, "The aeroplane has made war so terrible that I do not believe any country will again care to start a war." Five years later, he had changed his mind and wrote, "The possibilities of the aeroplane for destruction by bomb and poison gas have been so increased since the last war that the mind is staggered in attempting to picture the horrors of the next one."

1921: First naval vessel sunk by aircraft

1940: First wartime use of military gliders

1941: More than three hundred Japanese planes attack the American naval base at Pearl Harbor, Hawaii. More than 2,300 Americans are killed.

1945: Thirteen hundred British and American bombers drop more than three thousand tons of bombs on Dresden, Germany, killing as many as 135,000 civilians. Atomic bombs are dropped on Hiroshima and Nagasaki, Japan, resulting in 130,000 casualties.

1948: First airplane hijacking

1977: At the time, the worst airline disaster in history: 582 people are killed when two Boeing 747s collide on a runway in the Canary Islands.

1985: When a Japan Airlines 747 crashes into a mountain, 520 people are killed.

1988: When a bomb explodes on a Pan Am Boeing 747 over Lockerbie, Scotland, 270 people are killed.

2001: Terrorists crash two commercial airliners into New
York City's World Trade Center towers, and another
into the Pentagon in Washington, and a fourth crashes
in Pennsylvania after passengers fight back. More than
3,000 people are killed.

"I don't have any regrets about my part in the invention
of the airplane, though no one could deplore more than I do the
destruction it has caused," wrote Orville Wright. "I feel about
the airplane much as I do in regard to fire. That is, I regret all
the terrible damage caused by fire. But I think it is good for the
human race that someone discovered how to start fires, and
that it is possible to put to thousands of important uses."

Spies in the Skies

According to several biographies of the Wright brothers, after
Augustus Herring spent a week at the Wright camp in 1902, he
went to Washington hoping to trade the secret of the flying
machine for a job at the Smithsonian Institution with Samuel
Langley. To his credit, Langley refused to meet with Herring.

But Langley was certainly interested in the Wrights. Three
days after Herring left Kitty Hawk, Langley wrote this to Octave
Chanute: "I should be glad to hear more of what the Wright
brothers have done, and especially of their means of control. . . .
I should be very glad to have either of them visit Washington at
my expense to get some of their ideas on this subject, if they are
willing to communicate them."

Two days later Langley sent a telegram to Wilbur Wright
asking permission to visit their camp. Wilbur turned him down.

That December, Langley wrote Chanute *again*, requesting

information about the Wrights' control system and inviting them to speak with him in Washington.

Then, in the fall of 1905, the Wrights were testing their new plane in Ohio when they noticed two men watching from a pasture. One man had a camera. He was Samuel Langley's chief engineer.

Langley died the next year, but in 1908 while Orville Wright was recovering in a hospital from a crash, Alexander Graham Bell (who was *also* trying to invent the airplane) and his associates went into Orville's hangar and took measurements of his plane.

But Augustus Herring was the main nemesis of the Wright brothers. A week after the Wrights' first successful flight in 1903, Herring wrote them a letter. According to Orville: "When we made our first power flight in 1903 he immediately wrote a letter suggesting that he could reveal our system of control and cause us a great deal of trouble and proposing that we give him a third interest in our invention." The Wrights ignored him.

Herring then took what he knew to Glenn Curtiss, another aviation pioneer. In 1921 Orville wrote: "Later he secured the controlling stock in the Curtiss Company by representing to Curtiss that he had a *photograph* which would defeat our patent" (the italics are mine).

So it is not bending the truth too much to suggest that Herring was a spy. However, the scene in which Johnny catches him photographing the flyer was invented.

Actually, the Wrights did a little spying of their own. In 1914 Orville sent his brother Lorin to spy on Glenn Curtiss. When he tried to take photos of a plane Curtiss was working on, Lorin Wright was caught and his film was confiscated.

What Happened to the First Airplane?

When it was wrecked after the fourth flight on December 17, 1903, the flyer was crated up and sent back to Ohio. It wasn't uncrated until 1916, when it was rebuilt. The plane was displayed at the Massachusetts Institute of Technology and then sent to the Science Museum of London in 1928. The flyer returned to America twenty years later. You can see it today at the National Air and Space Museum in Washington, D.C. (where the author's photo at the end of this book was taken).

When the flyer was finally unveiled at the Smithsonian, one of the honored guests was Johnny Moore, who was sixty-three years old. When reporters asked him why he'd barely glanced at the flyer, he said, "I seen it before."

One last thing . . .

The Chicago Cubs *did* win the World Series in 1908, and as every Cub fan knows, they haven't won it since that year. But as the Wright brothers demonstrated, *anything* is possible.

Read More!

If you want to learn more about the Wright brothers, look in your library for these books for young people.

Freedman, Russell. *The Wright Brothers: How They Invented the Airplane.* New York: Scholastic, 1991.

Glines, Carroll V. *The Wright Brothers: Pioneers of Power Flight.* New York: Franklin Watts, 1968.

Haynes, Richard M. *The Wright Brothers.* Englewood Cliffs, N. J.: Silver-Burdett Press, 1991.

King, Dorothy. *The Wright Brothers: The Story of the Conquest of the Air.* London: Blackie & Son, 1958.

Marquardt, Max. *Wilbur and Orville and the Flying Machine.* Austin: Raintree Steck-Vaughn, 1992.

Parker, Steve. *The Wright Brothers and Aviation.* New York: Chelsea House Publishers, 1995.

Quackenbush, Robert. *Take Me Out to the Airfield! How the Wright Brothers Invented the Airplane.* New York: Parents' Magazine Press, 1976.

Reynolds, Quentin. *The Wright Brothers.* New York: Random House, 1981.

Ruehrwein, Dick. *Discover the Wright Brothers and Flight.* Greendale, Ind.: The Creative Company, 1995.

Sabin, Louis. *Wilbur and Orville Wright: The Flight to Adventure.* Mahwah, N.J.: Troll Associates, 1983.

Schulz, Walter A. *Will and Orv.* Minneapolis: Carolrhoda Books, 1991.

Sobol, Donald J. *The Wright Brothers at Kitty Hawk.* New York: Scholastic, 1961.

Sproule, Anna. *The Wright Brothers: The Story of the Struggle to Build and Fly the First Successful Aeroplane.* Toronto: Irwin Publishing, 1991.

Stevenson, Augusta. *Wilbur and Orville Wright: Young Fliers.* New York: Aladdin, 1986.

Woods, Andrew. *Young Orville and Wilbur Wright: First to Fly.* Mahwah, N.J.: Troll Associates, 1992.